MODEL

MARINE

Sondra Sykes Meek

Sondra Sykes Meek

ISBN-10: 1548687278
ISBN-13: 978-1548687274
Library of Congress Control Number: 2017919702
LCCN Imprint Name: CreateSpace Independent Publishing Platform, North Charleston, SC

*To my brothers and sisters of the armed forces.
May your sacrifices never be forgotten.*

Contents

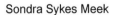

Acknowledgments

Thank you to my family, friends, and colleagues who read and edited my initial drafts. I couldn't have done this without your support.

Special thanks to Pat Conroy, who before he passed, reminded me I'm "a novelist" and encouraged me to tell this story.

Characters

Molly Monroe: Main character

Nick Monroe: Molly's brother

Donna Monroe: Molly's mother

Beth Bailey: Molly's high school friend

Sergeant Brian Price: Molly's co-worker

Lance Corporal Vanessa Ramirez: Molly's best friend

Sergeant Andrew Hicks: Alpha Company Marine

Private First Class Dakota Hart: Alpha Company Marine

Corporal Trinity Baptiste: Molly's friend on the Female Engagement Team

Lieutenant John Michaelson: Nick Monroe's best friend and the Alpha Company Platoon Commander

Prologue

Corporal Molly Monroe

He had introduced himself as Brian Price. He said, "I brought you some pictures to help you remember what good friends we are." She had sensed there was more to his statement than his light-hearted tone suggested. She hadn't remembered his name, but she had been drawn to him. She had felt something when she woke and saw him sleeping in his wheelchair next to her. It was as if someone had covered her with a warm blanket of calm. She had felt momentarily insulated from the horrors that plagued her dreams.

She was sitting upright in her hospital bed, the left side of her face swathed in bandages. He sat in his wheelchair to her right, as close to her as the equipment would allow him, with pictures spread out across the sheets on her lap. She enjoyed his slow Tennessee twang as much as the stories he told her. She had watched his smile deepen the lines around his mouth and eyes and accentuate the dimple on his right cheek. He had shown her a picture of herself riding a mechanical bull, and when he told her that it was his favorite picture of her, she believed him.

He picked up a picture of three female Marines in desert uniforms, rifles slung over their right shoulders, walking past rows of tan tents. "This is one of my better candid shots from Camp Leatherneck, I think," he said.

Two of the Marines were engaged in an animated conversation. He pointed to a pretty Latina with expressive brown eyes. She appeared to be speaking with her hands out in front of her, fingers spread wide, in a gesture that indicated something big.

"This is Lance Corporal Ramirez. You two have been besties since boot camp," he said.

Then he pointed to the Marine walking next to Ramirez, with skin as dark as a starless night, her right hand held firmly to her rifle strap, left hand over her heart, and her face in the throes of laughter. "This is Corporal Baptiste. You met her in Afghanistan, and we all became friends pretty quickly. You loved her lyrical voice, whether she was telling bayou ghost stories or singing her favorite gospel hymns."

Then he pointed to Molly herself: the Marine with blond French-braided hair and blue eyes, walking slightly to the left, a couple of steps behind Corporal Baptiste — the only one of the three who seemed to have noticed the photographer. Her expression was grim, angry even. "Yeah, as you can see, you weren't too happy with me that day," he said.

Molly looked at Brian, trying to read his expression. "Why was I mad at you?"

"You wanted to go on a mission with the Alpha Company Marines, and I had given the mission to one of the other troops instead."

The thought didn't stir any anger in her now, and Molly wasn't sure what to think about that, so she let it go. There was another picture in the pile that attracted her attention, but it was out of her reach. She pointed to it and said, "What about that one?"

He picked up the one with several Marines standing together in a pose. "Lance Corporal Ryan took this one. He works with us. These are several of the Alpha Company Marines. Our team spent a lot of time with their unit. They did some pretty cool stuff out there."

There were about twenty Marines in their desert cammies standing grouped together in their battle rattle, with an assortment of weaponry. They all looked ready for a mission. Brian was going through the names as he had with the other pictures, but his voice became a hum in her ears, as her open right eye was drawn to the lieutenant, who stood front and center of the group with a high and tight haircut and hazel eyes.

She felt something trigger in her chest. Her heartbeat accelerated. She knew who he was. She had known him well before she joined the Corps, but that was years ago. She could not understand why he was in this picture. She remembered a beach and officer quarters, and goose bumps erupted on her arms and her legs as flashes of passion teased her flesh. And then Brian pointed to another Marine and said, "Here's Sergeant Hicks…"

Molly looked at the muscular Marine with red hair, freckles, and a sunburn and felt her heart lurch in her throat. She did not recognize him, but she was seized with fear. She thought she knew him but could not recall his name or how she knew him. His face frequented her nightmares. She closed her eyes as frightening images flooded her mind. She began to hyperventilate. "Stop!" she yelled. "Put it away!" She felt like she might throw up.

"Oh geez, I'm so sorry, Molly. I don't know what I was thinking." He gathered all the pictures together and placed them on the table. He stroked her exposed cheekbone and said, "We'll talk about something else, okay?"

Her voice was caught in her throat. There was a lump that she couldn't swallow. She nodded and squeezed his hand.

He leaned back in his wheelchair and smiled at her, his thumb gently caressing her wrist. "I doubt you remember this, but I was on duty the day you checked in to the company."

She watched him as she waited for him to continue. His brown eyes were fixed on something in the distance. His relaxed features and crooked smile revealed his amusement. She wished she remembered more about herself as a Marine, but for the moment, she only had disjointed, fragmented recollections.

"You looked so sharp in your service uniform," he said.

His devilish grin and dimples were completely distracting. She could feel herself smiling despite her gnawing anxiety and growing weariness. "Okay. So what did I do? Did I trip or something? I must have done something silly for you to sit there looking so full of yourself."

He said, "Oh no. You were quite composed and dignified. Very squared away actually."

She could tell he was teasing her, and she intuitively understood that must be a natural characteristic of their friendship.

He finally erupted in laughter: "All except for your ribbons...you had two then, and they were on backward!"

Molly smiled and closed her eyes. "Oh. That's not very squared away," she said.

He responded. He was reassuring her, she could tell, but she didn't catch his words: only his smooth, silky voice. She held on to it as she faded into slumber.

"If thou didst ever hold me in thy heart,

Absent thee from felicity awhile,

And in this harsh world draw thy breath in pain,

To tell my story."

William Shakespeare, *Hamlet*, 5.2

Butterfly

Molly Monroe

Molly smiled at the yellow and brown flower floating in her dirty pudgy palms. "Oh no, it's waving good-bye," she realized too late, as the butterfly fluttered away. "Don't go," she whispered. She left her plastic shovel and bucket in Mama's garden so she could run along with her flittering friend. The early-morning sun tickled her skin, and the air was as wet as the dewy grass. The soft green blades squished delightfully between her toes; she giggled and imagined Mama's face if she could see Molly running around outside in her nighty and bare feet. She moved like a ballerina, dancing and twirling, with her winged partner above her. She leaned and swayed as her white-blond hair billowed pale silk in the wind, her body bending in fluid motions with the sparrows' song, oblivious to the butterfly's lethal course.

When she heard her father holler in the distance, the sound blended with the jumping, thumping crickets and toads. "Run, Nicky, Run!" She didn't hear the words or the fear in her daddy's voice. She didn't hear the whirr of the cars as they sped by a few short feet in front of her. She only heard the rhythm of a deep crescendo, and it matched the tempo of her dance, urging her to spin faster, soar higher — beautiful like a butterfly — until something sent her crashing to the ground; a violent force that stole her breath and stopped the music.

Then the sounds of a thundering horn and a screech of brakes reached her ears, and then, the deep bellow of an engine resuming its speed, as eighteen wheels stayed on course, twenty-three inches beyond her blond mane. She looked up into the round brown eyes of her big brother, who had her pinned in the dewy soft grass. "I got you, baby girl," he said, with a goofy red smile that exposed a missing front tooth.

Nick Monroe

The red numbers glared at him in the dark. When they finally rolled over to four o'clock, he got out of bed. There was no sense in pretending to sleep anymore. After a tense evening, unable to comfort his mom, he had tried convincing her—and himself—to get some rest. They had a long day ahead of them.

He didn't bother with the lights as he quietly slipped on his shirt, pants, and shoes in his old, familiar bedroom. He stuffed his wallet in his pocket and picked up the large manila envelope on his nightstand, intending to go to the kitchen to reread the letter inside.

Instead, he found himself in Molly's old bedroom. The moonlight shining through the large bay window welcomed him. He walked past her bed on the near wall, toward the bookshelf that dominated the room. It was overflowing with the books she had loved; it was brimming with classics. She had a section set aside for Shakespeare and another for stage plays, but most of the shelves were stacked with ragged copies of her favorite fiction, titles such as *Wuthering Heights, Anna Karenina*, and *To Kill a Mockingbird*.

He slumped in the chaise by the window; her room was soothing. A framed newspaper clipping hung above her dresser: a three-year-old critique of her performance as Juliet with the Tampa troupe in their spring production of *Romeo and Juliet*. He scanned the wall above her bed. Beauty-pageant sashes and framed newspaper articles with her "Little Miss" and "Teen Miss" wins covered the walls.

He had been so proud of her. He was just her brother, but he often felt like he had been more of a father to her.

His mom must still be burning Molly's candles in here, he realized. Molly and her room had always smelled like a fruit basket. She obsessed over her lotions and candles. He had teased her pretty hard about it when she was younger, but his words hadn't fazed her. She was serious when she said, "The sense of smell is even more important than the sense of sight, Nicky. It doesn't matter how great you look. If you stink, nobody wants to be around you." She scrunched her nose. "By the way, when was the last time *you* showered?" He grinned. He had laughed when he learned how much time she had to spend with stinking men in the sweltering heat all day. The irony of it got the best of him. Even though she had become much tougher in the last couple of years, she was still 100 percent girl. She had sent him the strangest e-mail a couple of months ago. If it hadn't been so scary, he might have been able to laugh about it.

Hey Nicky,

How's Ma holding up? Is she over it yet? I hope so. She can't stay mad at me forever, can she?

So, the craziest thing happened a couple of days ago. We were hit with mortars around 3AM. Scared the hell out of me. I heard shrill sounds slicing through the air above me. When they landed, the BOOMs rattled my cot, and I could have sworn they had destroyed our camp. It turns out they actually landed about a mile away. No one was hurt. But it sure was a crazy wake-up call. I had my helmet and flak on before my uniform! LMAO. Anyway, other than the scare, no big deal. I was fine. Just a minor case of the shakes.

Anyway, this place stinks. I mean literally! Can you please send me some scented lotions? My skin is as dry as sandpaper, and I really need to clear the smell of raw sewage, burning rubber, and plain ole B.O. from my nose. Please? I'll love you forever.

He still wasn't used to this version of his sister. He did not understand how she could be so cavalier about war. *LMAO?* Really?

Daybreak chased away the shadows, and he was drawn to the two framed photos on her dresser. They were newer than most of the other pictures in the room. He liked the five-by-seven frame of the two of them. It was taken the day of her high-school graduation, when the sun had been intense. Her cheeks were flushed pink, and her eyes were bright blue, in stark contrast to his dark-brown eyes, olive complexion, and dark-brown hair. She was thin like Ma, but Molly was almost as tall as he was. She was a paler version of him. You could tell they were siblings because their angular features, full lips, and long lashes were the same. She was smiling in this picture, the same naïve smile she had most of her life.

But those innocent days were long gone. The picture next to it was evidence that her old way of life had been permanently replaced by a new one. It represented the drastic turn of events more than two years earlier. She had chosen a role that seemed completely wrong for her. He picked up the frame and studied her stern expression. She was not smiling. Her hair was pulled back in a tight braid. Her posture was rigid. She wore a dress blue uniform and a white hat with a glossy black rim that displayed a brass emblem with an eagle, globe, and anchor. She looked the part of "The Few. The Proud." He had to admit that much.

She wore her uniform like it was a coat of armor. But Nick was sure that damned uniform would be the death of their Molly, whether she lived through this or not.

He pulled a picture out of his wallet. He had carried it with him since the day he had picked it up from Walgreens nearly three years before. It was a snapshot of him and his best friend, John, with their girlfriends. Back then, he had thought at least one of those couples would have been married by now.

He sat down on Molly's bed and pulled out his last letter from John.

Nick,

Thanks for letting me know she was headed over here. She still doesn't know where I am, but I suspect she's going to figure it out eventually. I've been doing what I can to keep her on the camp, but she's not making it easy for me. You know as well as I do how stubborn she has become! I'll keep you posted.

On another note: Just in case...I have a letter for her in this package. If anything happens to me, please make sure she gets it. But don't even think about that, bro. Three months down. Four to go. I'm telling you, the days fly by here. Before we know it, we'll be grilling steaks, drinking beer, and planning our next road trip. I'm thinking somewhere cold and scenic. I've had my fill of the sand and heat for a while!

What do you think about Colorado? I hear Steamboat is a great place to go skiing. Think about it. I'll be in touch.

Nick put the letter down. The sun had risen, and the summer heat was already burning through the large bay window. His chest constricted, and his throat tightened. Sweat formed on his forehead. The humidity was swallowing him. And the grief weighed down on him.

Damn, he needed a drink.

Donna Monroe

Donna was a creature of habit. She had walked the streets of her neighborhood every morning from five to six o'clock for all her adult life. But this morning, she didn't notice the elephant ears, great oaks, and blue jays she adored. It had been seventeen years since she had lost her husband, Matthew, and she had forgotten how quickly a life could be turned upside down.

She had held herself together until Nick had finally arrived last night. They had watched the evening news together, and then she had crumbled. He had held her firmly for what must have been hours while she cried the tears she had tried to contain. She had fallen into a dreamless sleep for a few hours but woke with bittersweet memories as fresh as the day they occurred.

Donna handed Molly the book.

"But, Ma, I did it already. And you said Beth could come over and play."

"She can come in a little while. You only practiced barefooted. Now you have to learn how to do it in heels. Put them on, and you'll see how different it is."

Molly squealed when she saw the shiny silver rhinestones on her new shoes. "Are these for me?"

Donna said, "Well, they don't fit my feet," and Molly giggled when Donna shoved her big toes into the little shoe. "Now go on. You want to win, don't you?"

Molly put on the high heels and placed the book on top of her head, walking in dignified circles around the kitchen table.

"That's it. Shoulders straight. Swing your leg from the hip."

After five minutes without dropping the book, Donna clapped her hands.

Molly curtsied with the book on her head and said, "I'm going to be Little Miss Sunshine, ain't I, Ma?"

"Aren't I," Donna corrected. "And yes, baby, I think you are."

Donna smiled. Molly had won, and Donna had felt the accomplishment as much as her daughter did. She treasured her memories of raising her children. Sometimes it had been hard, but she had felt fortunate that her job as a teacher had been so conducive to motherhood. She had been an involved mom, and she believed that her guidance had set her children up for happy and successful futures. She supposed that was why the last couple of years had been so difficult. All along she had believed that she and Molly agreed on what was best for her, and then Molly completely changed direction. No North Carolina School of the Arts. No explanation. No apology.

Why wouldn't Donna have been bitter about it?

She had finished her walk three days ago with fresh ideas for her students, but she had arrived home to hear a cryptic yet disturbing message on her answering machine. She had returned the call, and everything after that had become a blur. The Marine on the phone had been kind and sympathetic. They had exchanged several phone calls in the last two days as Molly's locations and prognoses had changed. At first, they thought Donna would be flying to Germany, but now she was flying to

DC. They had helped her make all the travel arrangements. They would be escorting Nick and her to the airport later this afternoon. She needed their assistance, and she resented it.

She hadn't spoken to Molly since her Christmas vacation. In fact, they had both been angry the last time Donna had seen her, and Molly had left several days earlier than planned.

"You know we don't belong in this war," Donna said.

"No. I don't know that. But I'm not trying to convince you otherwise, Ma."

"You've become erratic, and I don't understand you anymore."

"I've changed. That's all. Quit being so dramatic."

"Can't you see they've brainwashed you!"

"What? I wanted this! Why won't you just accept it? You can go on believing whatever the hell you want. It's your constitutional right! But quit trying to deter me from mine!"

"Watch your language, young lady! And listen to me…"

"I listened to you for eighteen years, Ma! But I guess you wouldn't call that brainwashing!"

She had slammed the door behind her.

Paying Respects

Corporal Molly Monroe

She sat on the hill with Ramirez, overlooking the Airboss tent. The desert stretched for miles across an endless horizon. The orange glow of the sun peeked over the sea of sand and sent violet and crimson streaks into the fading night sky. It reminded her of another time, when the sea was ocean instead of sand — when love rekindled and then withered again. She marveled at the natural beauty of a place that was so perilous.

"Thanks for coming with me," Ramirez said.

"Of course. I'm glad you brought me along," Monroe said. "Will they be here soon?"

"Any minute. I prepared the last one for this flight a couple hours ago."

"I can't imagine having your job, Ramirez. Does it ever get to you?"

"I try to detach myself. You know how that goes. But sometimes, they look so young. I can't help thinking about my kid brother. I can't help imagining what their families are going through. Sometimes, it starts to feel like I know them."

Two Humvees approached the flight line and parked; the Marines inside waited for their cue.

The CH-53 helicopter roared to life, the rotating blades sending desert dust particles funneling around the gray bird. The Marines exited their vehicles and pulled the large black bag out of the back. Placing it on a field-expedient stretcher, they somberly carried their brother up the ramp, into the belly of the bird. They showed no sense of urgency, as they repeated the slow procession from the Humvee to the helo two more times. On their final trip out of the helicopter, the Marines formed a line from a distance. As the bird began ascent of the Angel Flight, Corporal Monroe and Lance Corporal Ramirez stood and joined their fellow warriors in a final salute.

Corporal Trinity Baptiste

"Hey, Baptiste, wake up. Let's go for a run."

Baptiste peeked her head out of the sleeping bag and looked at her clock. It was 0445, and the tent was still as cool as a Popsicle. The AC worked like a gem at night but was much less effective in the heat of the day. As much as she loved running and the morning glory of sunrise, she had returned to the camp late the night prior and needed her sleep. "What?"

"I said, let's go for a run," Monroe said.

"Girl, did ya see what time I got in? No, you didn't, 'cause ya was sleeping! Now go away; I have a mission later."

"What? You do? You have to tell me about it!"

Dear Lord, give me patience with this child, Baptiste thought. "Girl, ya betta get away from me!"

"Oh, come on, don't you want to see the sunrise?" Monroe pleaded.

In response, Baptiste zipped her sleeping bag all the way up so that her face was covered. She heard Monroe sigh and walk away, and then she heard her wake up Jankowski, Baptiste's Female Engagement Team partner. *She was prolly gonna interrogate her about today's mission,* Baptiste thought. *Good. Ski needs the PT anyway.*

Sergeant Brian Price

Sergeant Price tapped his foot to Keith Urban's "I'm In," which was streaming through the earpiece tucked in his left ear as he flipped through the images on his computer screen. He enjoyed seeing what was going on outside the camp from his air-conditioned tent. Not that he avoided going outside the wire—he just didn't go unless it was necessary. Lance Corporal Ryan wasn't the best photographer on his team, and his articles were average, but he was improving. He got the job done though, so Sergeant Price had what he needed for his next submission to higher headquarters.

When the phone rang, Corporal Monroe jumped to answer it, but he beat her to it. He had seen an e-mail on this mission already, so he was expecting the call. "Combat Camera, Sergeant Price speaking." He wrote down the essentials as his customer spoke, and then he said, "Sure thing. He'll be there in five minutes."

Sergeant Price hung up the phone. "Lance Corporal Ryan, get over here!"

Lance Corporal Ryan was on the far side of the tent studying the layout of their latest article, while some metal band blared from his computer speakers.

"Ryan!" Sergeant Price yelled.

Ryan jumped, and his rifle clunked against the plywood floor.

"You owe me ten for that, Devil Dog!"

Ryan grabbed his weapon and shuffled to the front of the sergeant's desk. "Yes, sergeant! Aye, sergeant!" Then he threw himself into the pushup position, with his M-16 rifle stretched across the top of his hands, and he counted each push-up aloud—since each Marine Corps push-up was a four-count exercise—two repetitions were counted as one. Lance Corporal Ryan counted, "One, two, three; *one!* One, two, three; *two!*" until he completed the twenty repetitions.

"Get on your feet."

Lance Corporal Ryan obeyed.

"Prepare your daypack and equipment. Alpha Company just requested you for a civil-engineering project at the clinic."

Sergeant Price was amused by the lance corporal's response. He hesitated long enough to glance at Corporal Monroe. They all knew she had wanted a mission outside the wire since they arrived, but none of them discussed the subject in front of her. Lance Corporal Ryan may have tried to look apologetic, but he was unable to conceal his excitement completely. "Aye, sergeant!"

But then Sergeant Price followed Ryan's gaze, and when he saw Monroe, he almost felt sorry for the kid. He watched her watching Ryan as the young Marine scrambled toward the tent opening. Her face was deadpan: she sat motionless except for those blue eyes of hers, which were as shocking as a lightning rod. She followed him with an aim that looked ready to kill. She didn't crack a smile at Ryan's awkward retreat, which was making it hard for Price to keep from laughing out loud at the kid. Ryan had enough enthusiasm for the whole damn platoon. He was like a doe-eyed buck:

innocent and skittish, but he was very muscular and had lethal strength. It cracked him up that such a pretty little thing like Monroe could intimidate a muscle head like Ryan. The kid pulled too hard on the zipper of the tent opening, and it got stuck midway. As he fidgeted with it, the desert sun penetrated the dimly lit area. Dust particles floated around his legs. The dog tag in his left boot reflected the sunlight against the interior of the canvas tent.

Monroe stood. "Just leave it alone, Ryan!"

Ryan ducked under the flap and nearly tripped on his way out.

"What's the problem, Monroe?" Sergeant Price said.

"As if you don't know."

Yeah, he knew. "It's not the kid's fault," he said.

"No. It's not! It's yours! Why do you let Alpha Company tell you who will go on a mission with them? That's not their place!"

He closed his eyes and inhaled. He was not going to let her get under his skin. "Why must you always question orders, Monroe? Last I checked, I'm in charge here." His voice was calmer than his gut. He didn't like her being angry with him, but he had to put his foot down, or no one would respect him. At least that was what he told himself, since they were the only two in the tent at the moment.

"Are you? Or is Alpha Company? I've missed three missions because of this crap! And I'm all about getting the kid trained, but why should I lose job credibility and combat experience just because you can't say no to them? This screams of high heaven of discrimination!"

"Are you accusing me of discrimination? Come on, Monroe; you know me better than that."

"No. I'm not accusing you of discrimination, but I am accusing them. And you're at fault because you haven't done anything to stop it. So here's the deal, Sergeant Price — if this happens again, I'm running it up the flagpole. I've heard the battalion commander's opinion of sexual discrimination, and I know he'll do something about it!" She grabbed her rifle and helmet and stormed toward the tent opening.

"Where are you going?" He was concerned about her. Some things needed to be left alone, and she was pushing it. Most of the time, Monroe acted professionally. But now, she was acting like a hothead, and she could get herself in trouble. He didn't understand her itch to venture outside the camp, and he wished she would just drop it.

"Alpha Company!" she shouted from outside, leaving the tent flap whipping in the wind.

It picked up force then, piling layers of fine beige dust on the plywood floor.

Sergeant Andrew Hicks

The seasoned Marines had dubbed the area beneath the camo netting "the House of Spades," and there they enjoyed the few hours of leisure before they went out on patrol again. The four Marines scarfed down their tasteless combat rations at the plywood table between the rounds of cards.

Sergeant Hicks adjusted himself on the milk crate. "It's your bid, Stinson."

Sergeant Stinson nodded and said, "We'll go five."

Sergeant Hicks responded in his embellished Texas drawl and with a long, slow exhale of his cigar fumes. "Well, I've got a Little Mo all by myself, so we'll play it safe and stick with that. You good with that, Carter?"

"Excuse me."

The sound of a female voice startled the Marines, and the game was abruptly forgotten. But it was the tone of her voice that caught Sergeant Hicks's attention. It wouldn't matter what words came out of her mouth: that girl was in a horn-tossing mood, and he knew it.

"I don't mean to interrupt," she said.

"But you did anyway," Sergeant Hicks responded. He didn't understand it, but her approach just pissed him off. She stood just outside the camo netting as if she expected one of the men to get up and greet her. It irked him that he was tempted to do such a thing himself. Even with her hair pulled back into the tight braid and no makeup, he had to admit that she was easy on the eyes. Most of the women Marines used their looks to their advantage, and he sure as hell wasn't going to allow her to do that to him or his men. Damn, if he could just open his mouth.

They all stared at her. And she stared back.

Finally, Murphy was the one who said, "Can I help you?"

"I'd like to speak with your platoon commander. I was hoping you could take me to him."

Sergeant Hicks stood. "I'm the platoon sergeant. How can I help you, Corporal?" He emphasized her rank when he spoke.

"I'd actually like to speak with your lieutenant, Sergeant."

"What do you need with him?" he asked.

He couldn't tell if she squinted from the sun or from good old-fashioned rage. "That's for me to discuss with him," she said.

Her eyes were about to burn right through him— he was sure. He didn't know what her problem was, but it didn't matter. He couldn't let her show him up in front of the other Marines. "Simmer down, Corporal. I don't know what brings you to Alpha Company or what you want with the lieutenant, but you won't get anywhere using that tone with me."

"You don't have *any idea* why I'm here?" She threw her hands on her hips when she spoke, and he decided right then and there that he didn't like her or that bigger 'n Dallas chip on her shoulder.

"Not a freakin' clue, your highness." Hicks glanced back at the others and rolled his eyes. "I guess we are supposed to know why—" he paused as he directed a dramatic stare at the name tape on her breast pocket—"Corporal Monroe here has graced us with her presence." He made a show of lowering himself down on one knee in a mock bow and rolling his right hand toward her feet.

When the others broke out in raucous laughter, he stood and joined them before turning to face the corporal. But when he looked in her direction, she was gone. That's when he realized they were laughing *at him.*

He stepped out of the shade just in time to see her entering the command tent.

That girl could start a fight in an empty house! He grunted to himself and tried to ignore the heat burning from his chest to his ears before taking off after her.

Unspoken

Molly Monroe

Molly swayed as fluorescent swirling patterns splashed across a wall of radiant color. Glowing sticks, swelling hearts, and supple limbs tangled in a luminous web of want, radiating the only light amid a span of darkness. A man with Mickey Mouse ears stood in front of a keyboard on stage. The electronic rhythm pulsed through a mass of balmy bodies in an exploration of life and each other.

As her eyes adjusted to the darkness beneath the flashing strobes, she discovered the sea of sinuous silhouettes. Buoyancy radiated the swell of bodies as they surged with the rhythm. Pink, yellow, and orange streamers swirled around smiling faces, providing flickering glimpses of supple, spectral shadows.

Her best friend had left her there alone. She was twenty miles from home with nothing but a few dollars in her pocket. Her purse was in the car. Her cell phone was in her purse. But she was not angry; the emotion was a distant ember no longer fueled by thoughts of betrayal. She did not understand the source of burgeoning bliss and exotic sensations soaring through her nor did she feel a reason to fight them.

She surrendered herself to the rhythmic pulse. Her waist, her arms, and her whole body throbbed with freedom and verve. She explored herself as though for the first time. And when the stranger joined her in the discovery, she did not resist.

Beth Bailey

"Oh my God, Nick. Is she going to...will she...be okay?"

"I don't know. She's in a coma. They said something about a subdural hematoma. But they haven't said much about how severe the damage to her brain is."

Beth didn't notice the phone still in her hand when she reached for her heart. Images of her childhood crushed her. She squeezed her eyes shut against the flood of emotion. She could feel her heart tightening as she remembered selling Girl Scout Thin Mints; roasting marshmallows at campfires; and spending their summers in swimming pools and camps for drama, gym, and dance. Beth had helped Molly prepare for every beauty pageant.

"We should be sisters," Molly said.

"I have an idea," Beth suggested.

"We could change our names?"

"No. That won't work. We'll just change them again when we get married. True bonds are in the blood."

"I hate blood!" Molly said.

"We have to."

"No, we don't! I'm going to love you forever, but I don't want to see or touch any blood!"

"Then we can't be sisters."

"C'mon, Beth. There's another way."

"There isn't."

A day later, Molly approached her with a sewing needle. "Just so you know. I wouldn't do this for anybody else in the world!"

Beth had known she meant it.

They had planned their lives around each other, and she couldn't remember a time she and Molly hadn't been inseparable — they had never had a fight last longer than a day — until that night.

They had believed graduation would be a new beginning. They had both been accepted to North Carolina School of the Arts, and they had schemed magnificent strategies for making it in "the big time." They had dreamed of a double wedding: best friends marrying best friends. Their dreams had seemed so attainable at the time.

Instead, their friendship had come to a screeching halt within hours of graduation, as well as their imagined futures.

"Beth!" Nick barked.

"I'm sorry," she whispered as she placed the phone next to her ear. She had so many questions, so many things she wanted to say, but she was struggling to breathe.

"I thought you would want to know," he said softly.

And then the line went dead.

Donna Monroe

She stood by the kitchen sink and washed the pill down with a tall glass of water. Although she had pretended to be lost in her own thoughts, her ears had been actively tuned in to her son's clipped conversation from the living room. He had been speaking with Beth on the phone, and even after the long separation, Donna was certain he was not over her.

She had not been able to find out what had happened between them. Nick and Molly evidently shared the same reason for cutting Beth out of their lives, but she had not been able to discover which one of them Beth had wronged. Maybe she had done something to hurt both of them. Donna knew it had something to do with the week they had spent at the beach after the girls' high-school graduation, but despite her many attempts at probing, neither of her children had opened up to her about it. It hurt her to be excluded from their confidences. And Donna had felt terribly awkward in the beginning when Beth had called her or stopped by to see her. Beth would try to find out anything she could about Nick and Molly, but Donna would only shake her head and say, "I'm sorry, hon. I don't know a thing." Beth never mentioned what happened either. And Donna was too polite to ask. When Beth left for college, Donna decided it didn't matter anymore. By then, she had other things to worry about, like whatever had made Molly run off to that recruiter. There were too many things she still did not understand.

"All set, Ma?"

Nick's voice so close to her ear startled her. "You scared the daylights out of me," she said, before kissing him on the cheek. "I didn't hear you come in."

"Stealth mode," he said. "Did you take your meds?"

She held her water glass up as if in a toast. "All set," she said, before placing it next to the sink.

"Good. Where are your bags?"

"Who were you talking to, hon?" She thought she would test the waters.

"No one, Ma. Now where's your stuff? We have a plane to catch."

Molly Marine

Recruit Molly Monroe

"Platoon, halt!"

Platoon 4003 was marching to the Branch Medical Clinic, but they stopped at the intersection of Boulevard de France and Santo Domingo Street, in an area known as main side of the Marine Corps Recruit Depot, Parris Island, South Carolina. Molly heard and sensed her location rather than saw it. The troops were herded from one location to the next solely by the commands of their drill instructors. They only saw their surroundings when the women warriors who led them granted them permission to look.

"Left, face!"

In unison, the all-female platoon executed a facing movement toward their senior drill instructor. When she called another command, "Rest!" the recruits assumed the more formal position of parade rest, with their feet one foot apart and their thumbs clasped in the small of their backs. Although they were still in close-order drill, the position of rest could allow movement and low conversational tones – but the recruits would not be permitted such a luxury. The only reason their instructor called them to "rest" instead of "at ease" was so that they could respond to her questions and commands.

"Eyeballs!"

"Snap!" The platoon shouted the word as their collective eyes turned toward Staff Sergeant Martinez, the senior member of their team of drill instructors. The recruits

were nearing the end of their first week as a platoon, and Molly had learned already that the drill instructors could make a classroom or a gym out of any location, at any time. It was disconcerting to not know which was to come, as one could be much more unpleasant than the other.

Staff Sergeant Martinez pointed to a bronze statue of a female Marine wearing a service uniform and staring off into the distance, the object of her gaze unseen. "This is the Molly Marine statue. As she stands with her binoculars and book in hand, she looks to the future and records the history of women Marines and their contributions to the battlefield and the nation. She represents the warrior spirit of the fewest and proudest of the world's greatest fighting force. She embodies virtue, compassion, and devotion to duty; she exemplifies honor, courage, and commitment. She places others above herself. And like every Marine, she is willing to pay the ultimate price for our freedoms. She represents the best in all women Marines. And for those of you who make it, I better never hear of you disgracing her. Do you hear me, Platoon 4003?"

"Yes, ma'am!"

"And among one of you – in less than twelve weeks from now – for those of you nasties who are trainable, for those of you who have the intestinal fortitude to complete recruit training, you will nominate one member of your platoon for the Molly Marine Award. Is that understood?"

"Yes, ma'am!"

"I can't hear you!"

"Yes, ma'am!"

"Pla – toon. Atten – tion…uh – right…face! For – ward…march!"

First Lieutenant John Michaelson

John had known when her unit arrived, and he had made damn well sure that they never crossed paths. But then she had marched into his office as if she owned the place, and he hadn't been ready for it. His troops had been trained to inform him of unexpected visitors, but they hadn't this time.

He might have appreciated her temporary loss of bearing if he hadn't been struggling so hard to control his own. He felt her initial rage, and watched the minuscule play of emotions over her face. Her left brow arched involuntarily, and she released a barely audible gasp. He hoped she was in as much turmoil as he was. Even though he had once enjoyed the hold she had on him, it brought him nothing but misery now.

As if the situation needed more tension, Sergeant Hicks bolted into the tent seconds behind her, plowing into her full force, pushing her into John's arms. He caught her, and that herbal scent of hers, and wished he could keep her there.

She righted herself quickly.

As Sergeant Hicks scrambled to his feet, the pale skin of his freckled face shaded from pink to red, blending with his high-and-tight half-inch long red hair that skimmed the surface of his skull. "Terribly sorry, sir. The corporal requested to speak to you, but she took off before I could..."

"Are you okay?" He was still looking at Molly, but it was Sergeant Hicks who answered.

"Yes, sir. I'm fine. Should I..."

"Go finish your chow, Sergeant. I'll deal with the corporal."

He watched Sergeant Hicks leave before turning his attention back to Molly. "How did you find me?"

She had regained her composure. Some might assume that her Marine Corps training had instilled an intense sense of bearing in her, but he knew better. It was her stage training, or her mother's. They were one and the same, as far as he could tell. She was completely unruffled now. She said, "What makes you think I was looking for you?"

"Oh. You weren't?"

Molly said, "No. How would I know where you are these days? I haven't heard from you in a year."

"So why are you here then?"

"To give the platoon commander a warning."

"You're kidding, right?"

"No. I came to say that I would take this to the battalion commander if the discrimination continued. This is the third mission I've been bumped from."

"Why are you calling it discrimination, Molly? There are rules. There will be several missions you won't be permitted to go on, and you're just going to have to deal with that. Women aren't allowed on most of the trips Alpha Company takes outside the wire."

"I'm Corporal Monroe now, right? And the mission you kicked me off today has the Female Engagement Team on it, so quit playing dumb already! You're trying to ruin my career!"

"Watch yourself, *Corporal!* You'll ruin your own damn career if you don't get your military courtesies in check. I'm an officer in the United States Marine Corps!"

"You have no right getting me knocked off missions, *sir*!"

"You have no right being here! How the hell am I supposed to function properly with you out here trying to play G.I. Jane!"

Lance Corporal Vanessa Ramirez

Lance Corporal Ramirez set her rifle against the bench at the smoke pit. "What are you doing with that thing in your mouth, *Corporal*?" Ramirez cupped her hands to block the wind as she lit her cigarette, hoping her friend didn't notice her ongoing frustration with Monroe's recent promotion to corporal.

Monroe opened her mouth to speak but coughed instead.

Ramirez laughed. She would never have expected to see Monroe smoking. Forget about cancer — smoking causes wrinkles. Beauty Queen shouldn't be having any of that. She sat next to Monroe on the bench. "Bad day?" she asked.

"I don't know. It's been kind of like that zero-dark-thirty mortar fire we had a while back. It wasn't as bad as I thought it would be. It just shook me up."

"They say what doesn't kill you makes you stronger." The Marine Corps–issued sunglasses Monroe was wearing shielded her eyes, but Ramirez heard the wavering in her voice and suspected Beauty Queen was trying not to cry. "Anyway, I don't understand why you let this stuff get to you. Every day I don't have to go outside the wire is a good day for me. I hear it sucks out there. You know?"

"No. I don't know, Ramirez."

"If you did what I did, you sure as hell would, and you would appreciate the fact that no one is *making* you go out there."

"I didn't join the Corps to hide behind some fence. I want to carry my own weight just like any other Marine."

"Carry your own weight? That's a load of crap. Our boys are getting blown to bits out there, and here you are acting like you have something to prove. You got a death wish? You kicked ass in boot camp. You've been meritoriously promoted. Hell, everyone knows you carry your own weight, so don't give me that."

"I don't have a death wish. I have a job to do! And I just want to live up to—"

"Not another word about that statue, Monroe. How many times do I have to tell you it was a recruiting tool? That shit they sell you in boot camp is a bunch of propaganda. Don't get me wrong—it's just dandy that you won the Molly Marine award, but get a grip already. She wasn't a real person!"

Monroe didn't respond. She was staring off toward tent city—the rows of tan tents that were home to the Marines on Camp Leatherneck.

Ramirez guessed that convo was over. "I heard you stormed out on Sergeant Price. Did you really go to Alpha Company?"

"Yeah."

"And?" Ramirez thought Molly might have had her ass handed to her, but she would have been stewing in the "injustice of it all" if she had been reprimanded.

No. It seemed like she was sad or shocked. She wasn't angry. Her quiet mood just wasn't meshing. There was definitely something brewing in that head of hers.

"Hey. Corporal Monroe. Yoo-hoo. I'm on the edge of my freakin' seat here."

Monroe threw the half-smoked cigarette in the butt can and picked up her rifle without answering. She stood and walked out of the pit.

Ramirez jumped up. *Geez, she's acting weird.* "Hey. Don't leave a sister hanging! What happened when you went to Alpha Company?"

Monroe stopped and stared at Ramirez as if she had heard her for the first time. "Oh. Nothing. I handled it. See ya later, okay?"

"Yeah. Sure." Ramirez watched her friend walk away. She knew Monroe well enough to know that something was going on, and she intended to figure out what it was.

Roller Coaster

Molly Monroe

"I can't believe I let you talk me into this," Molly said. She gripped the shoulder restraint and concentrated on shutting down the tremors in her arms and legs. She visualized placing a serene mask over her face and took slow, steady breaths. She told herself she was relaxing.

"I can't believe I've been trying since the seventh grade to get you here. You must be the only high-school senior within ten miles of Busch Gardens who's never been on a roller coaster," Beth laughed as she spoke. "You need to live a little."

"I live a lot, thank you very much!" She looked out at the long lines of people and wondered if they saw the fear inside her or the fearless girl she wanted them to see. It doesn't matter what they think, *she thought.* They don't know me. *She closed her eyes to them, the shrinking trees, and the rest of the amusement park as their cart continued its two-hundred-foot climb.*

Beth said, "No, honey. You only pretend to live...on stage."

Molly opened her mouth to disagree, but then the bottom fell out from under her.

Beth Bailey

She pulled the shoeboxes out from under her bed and blew off the dust. She had left a couple of albums out in the apartment, but most of their childhood and teenaged memories were stuffed in shoeboxes.

Beth stared at the Busch Gardens picture of them on SheiKra. She had snuck over to the counter and bought it when Molly was in the restroom and had never even mentioned it to her. She studied the look on Molly's face. That look of raw fear was one of the few times that she had ever seen what was really going on inside her best friend. It was odd how Beth had needed that picture. She had needed to know that Molly had real emotions, and that she had been on that ride because of Beth. That she had been terrified but had gone there because Beth had asked her, well, begged her to go with her.

Molly was such a good actress. Beth had often wondered what was real and what wasn't with her. She saw how she placated her mother and then kept so much of her life a secret from her. Donna hadn't known that John and Molly were dating, and Beth had not understood why it had to be a secret, even after Nick explained their reasons to her. And then there were secrets that Molly kept from John. And Nick. And Beth had been her loyal friend, even after she and Nick broke up. And what did that get her? *Nothing.* Molly had stormed out of her life anyway.

Beth had hundreds of pictures of them together. Didn't that mean something? How could Nick drop a few bits of information like that and just hang up the phone? He hadn't spoken to her in two years, and now this? Did he think she had no heart? Or was he *trying* to hurt her? What about their eleven inseparable years together?

He would have been kinder to a complete stranger.

She caressed a picture of the three of them.

Nick had come home from JV football practice, dropped his duffel bag by the door, and plopped himself between Beth and Molly on the couch. Molly scrunched her nose and scooted away from him, but Beth inhaled deeply and wished she could move closer.

"Ewww, you need a shower," Molly said to Nick.

"What are you watching?"

"Kenneth Branagh's Hamlet. *It's the best of all the movie versions." Beth took her eyes off the television screen and looked at him when she spoke, resisting the urge to touch him. That they were interested in each other as more than friends was still a secret, and she didn't want to blow it.*

"Shhh, this is one of my favorite parts," Molly said.

Nick looked at the scene on the television. "This is your favorite part? The dude is talking to a skeleton's head beside an open grave."

"Hamlet is contemplating the death of a dear childhood companion," Molly said with a sniffle.

Nick shook his head. "That's great you understand what he's saying, because I don't think anybody else does."

"Shhh," Molly chided.

"No. I won't shhh...you two are morbid. Now come give me a hug!" He winked at Beth and tackled Molly, pleased with his sister's protests of disgust. Beth jumped in and tangled herself in their arms as the three of them became a rolling, twisting pretzel of laughter.

But nearly as quickly as it started, Molly fell off the couch and hit her head on the coffee table, and blood gushed from her scalp. Molly touched the back of her head, felt the sticky, wet, warm mass of hair, and almost passed out when she looked at her bloody hand. Beth cradled Molly's upper body and told jokes about her accident-prone friend while Nick applied first-aid and reminded Molly that head cuts bleed the worst — she didn't need stitches.

Beth had known as soon as Molly enlisted that this was a possibility. But she had not worried about it, nor had she concerned herself with watching the news. As far as she knew, they didn't send women into combat, and the Middle East had seemed like some distant, screwed-up place that resulted in price hikes at the gas pump. The war was just something for politicians to argue about. She had no passion for arguing over things she couldn't control — and the infamous "war on terror" had definitely been one of them.

She didn't pay much attention to the magnetic yellow ribbons people displayed on their cars. And she looked the other way when she saw the amputees with military haircuts. She wasn't trying to be cruel, but the thought of losing a limb was just sickening. God knows she had ignored her fair share of amputees in North Carolina.

But now, it was sinking in: her Molly, her best friend since second grade, was a — *what was that term everybody used?* — "wounded warrior." And the dominoes of this moment seemed to lead right back to her.

"I'm going to the lounge. You want me to get you some?" Jen said.

"Yeah!" Beth said.

"What about her?" Jen nodded in Molly's direction.

Beth discretely shook her head "no" and said, "I'll take Molly to get drinks."

Beth led Molly toward the closest bar, and Jen headed to the partitioned space on the other side of the building. Beth kept her eyes on Jen and noticed when Buddy intercepted her.

"What's that girl's name again?" Molly asked.

"Jen!" Beth had to holler over the music.

"When'd y'all become friends?"

"We aren't really," Beth said. "She's just a girl I met here."

"Where's she going?" Molly asked.

"I think she's just looking for her date," Beth said. But she knew better. Buddy had the goods, and they were going to the lounge to make the trade.

Beth hadn't meant to forget about Molly. She hadn't expected Buddy to drug her. She hadn't expected anything that had come next. And she was sorry. She was so, so sorry.

Shot Ex

Recruit Molly Monroe

"Blouses off!"

The recruits removed and folded their camouflage blouses so that their name tapes were showing and placed them neatly on the grass as if their uniforms were in formation. Then they situated their war belts on top of their blouses, keeping one canteen in their left hands. They stacked their weapons so that the rifles resembled waist-high pyramids next to the utility-blouse formation.

"Five, four, three, two, one! You're done! Give me two gear-guards. Now!"

Molly wasn't quick enough. Two other recruits claimed their posts watching the weapons and gear.

They had been drilling all morning on the Fourth Battalion parade deck, and her utility trousers were still damp with low-country humidity and recruit stench; her green T-shirt was darkened and dewy over her bra and armpits. At first, the cold blast of air was refreshing. But the sterile scent of the Branch Medical Clinic that accompanied it chilled her clammy skin as she tried to control the trembling that seized her limbs.

They entered the building single file and were led to a large room with beige walls; shiny, stainless-steel tables covered with medical supplies; a stainless-steel double-door refrigerator; three elementary-school-style desks; and thick blue mats covering the white-tiled deck. The Navy corpsmen —

the Marines' field medics — were wearing lab coats. The smell of their thin rubber gloves permeated the air.

The drill instructors gave directions for filling the mat, placing the recruits once again in columns and rows — softly, quietly, with no sounding off allowed in the building.

They sat cross-legged on the mats and listened to the petty officer in charge.

But Molly didn't hear the instructions. Her ears were buzzing, and she was trying to stop trembling. She took a swig of water from her canteen.

The petty officer walked toward a table, put on her gloves, and pointed to the row in front of her. The recruits stood and walked single-file to two corpsmen on the far-left side of the room. Each recruit stopped between the corpsmen long enough to receive a shot in each arm before walking toward the far-right corner of the room, where the three school desks were sitting two feet apart from one another; a corpsman faced each desk. Each recruit would sit, stare at the beige wall in front of her, and, without looking the corpsman in the eyes, present her veins as instructed.

And then it was Molly's row.

She stood, turned left, and followed Maye, the recruit in front of her. Molly focused on seeing nothing else around her. She studied the girl's short, black, frizzy hair. It was thick and damp; there were speckles of sand clumped in with the wet strands, and she recalled their trip to the sandpit that morning. The senior had IT'd — which meant "incentive training," but really meant punishment for — the whole platoon. Staff Sergeant Martinez had been disgusted with their drill practice and had double-timed them to the sandpit herself — thrashing them with push-ups, side-straddle hops, mountain climbers, flutter kicks, running in place, and leg lifts; changing instructions so quickly, the recruits flopped *around like fish. Molly was sure it must be comical to watch. But it was hell to be in the sandpit.*

As she drew closer to the corpsmen waiting to give her shots, she heard Ramirez whisper behind her, "Suck it up, buttercup!"

The prick near each of her shoulders happened so quickly she barely even felt them.

And then she sat in the desk. Her heartbeat in her ears, she tried to think of something besides the foot-long rubber band being wrapped around her arm, but all her eyes had to focus on was the dime-sized gray spot under the chipped beige paint on the wall in front of her. She squeezed the rubber ball when instructed and beckoned her old friend...

"It will have blood, they say; blood will have blood," she thought.

"Give thy thoughts no tongue..." the Bard countered.

She glanced at the hand as it released one vile of blood from the needle and inserted another tube. "The very substance of the ambitious is merely the shadow of a dream," she whispered, as a swirling purple tunnel swept across her vision.

"Speak up, recruit. Do you have a question?" She heard the corpsman's voice echoing in the distance.

"No, ma'am," she thought she heard herself say.

She didn't feel a thing when her head hit the desk.

Lance Corporal Vanessa Ramirez

Ramirez sat on her cot unlacing her boots. She shared the tent with about forty other females from the division. They all worked in different areas of the camp, but they shared a tent together because they were all female sergeants and below from the same unit — except for her. She was the only female Marine with Mortuary Affairs, so they had bunked her here with the other women. She was glad about that, since Molly stayed here too.

The male Marines were also grouped by rank and unit, but for the most part, they lived with guys from their same sections. Her own platoon shared a tent next to the Mortuary Affairs hut where they worked, and most of the time, she was awfully glad she had a reason to get away from the hut. There were times she was convinced it was haunted. She didn't care much for being excluded from the camaraderie of her platoon, but she was a realist. She believed that would never change. It wouldn't matter where she lay her head at night.

She was watching the two Female Engagement Team Marines argue a few cots down.

"Good Lord, Ski! Give me that!" Corporal Baptiste said as she snatched the chocolate-chip cookie out of Jankowski's hand.

"Ah, c'mon, Corporal. You need to chillax! One cookie's not gonna kill me."

Corporal Baptiste walked to the tent opening and threw it in the trash container outside. "No, but the company gunny will when we get stateside if ya don't quit stuffin' ya face. You're gonna get yourself thrown on weight control if ya keep it up."

Ramirez laughed. She and Monroe had taken a liking to Corporal Baptiste. She had the ability to speak the hard truth without being mean about it. It was all in her delivery. She could make an insult sound kind. Ramirez admired that about her and wished she knew how to do that. Ramirez was blunt by nature but had no idea how to soften the blow of her words.

Ramirez had heard one of the male Marines start mooing to one of his buddies when Jankowski walked by a few days ago. She got the joke—it was funny if you thought about it—but females around this joint had to stick together. "Hey, Ski, I'll run with you if you need a PT partner," she said.

"Thanks, Ramirez, but Corporal Monroe was gonna go out with me when she gets back."

"That's cool. I'll join you. We run the same pace anyway," Ramirez said.

"Great! I guess that means I'm going too," Corporal Baptiste chimed in. "I'm sure I'll be the one picking up Ski when she can't keep up."

"Hello. I'm standing right here!" Jankowski said.

Corporal Baptiste laughed. "Lighten up, Ski; I can't keep up with Monroe and Ramirez either. They act like every run is a race or something."

Ramirez smiled. She liked being fast. And she liked running with Monroe because it was always a challenge, and Ramirez usually beat her, especially when they ran in the sand.

"Where is she anyway?" Ramirez asked.

"She's still out on some convoy with the Alpha Company Marines. She has a lot more work outside the wire lately," Jankowski said.

"Yeah. Pretty much since she marched off in a tizzy to see that platoon commander in Alpha Company," Ramirez thought out loud.

"She's gone out with us on one mission. And she's supposed to go out with us again tomorrow. But there have been others too," Corporal Baptiste said.

Ramirez wondered if Molly had told them anything. She hadn't said much to her about it, and it was starting to get under her skin. "Any idea what she said to their lieutenant?"

"Not a clue," said Corporal Baptiste. "All I know is she asked us a million questions about the Female Engagement Team before she went to Alpha Company, so I'm guessing she knew she had been excluded from missions that women were on. She prolly told him she was fixin' to take her concerns up the chain of command. Prolly scared some sense into 'im."

That was what Ramirez thought too. "What do you guys do out there anyway?" Ramirez asked.

"Why? Ya ready to volunteer, girl?" Corporal Baptiste said.

"Uh, no. I won't go outside the wire unless somebody makes me. I'm not in as big a hurry to bite the bullet as you guys. You gonna tell me what you do or what?"

"We talk to the local women. They don't trust the male Marines. Hearts and minds can't be won if they won't talk to ya," Corporal Baptiste said.

"Well, that disqualifies me anyway," said Ramirez. "I don't speak the language."

Jankowski started laughing, and Corporal Baptiste snorted and said, "Bless ya heart, m'dear! We have our own 'terps!"

Ramirez felt her face get hot. Then she heard explosions.

Sergeant Andrew Hicks

He scanned the dirt terrain with vigilance. He had been in enough skirmishes to know they would come when you least expected them.

"Keep your eyes on the road, Hart," he said to his driver.

"Aye, Sergeant," PFC Hart said.

Sergeant Hicks looked out the passenger-side window to hide a smirk. As much as Monroe pissed him off, he had started to respect her. The girl would charge hell with a bucket of ice water to get outside the wire. And he couldn't really blame PFC Hart for sneaking peeks in the rearview mirror. She was very distracting. He scanned the desert terrain and was surprised when he caught sight of the two Ospreys several klicks to the south. They descended out of nowhere into the clear blue sky, and he watched as they made the transition from airplane mode to helicopter mode. He wondered why he didn't see any air-support escorts with them. *Damn, they must have been hauling ass! The Cobra helicopters probably couldn't keep up.* He didn't see any Harriers either. *Interesting.*

He let his thoughts wander and stole a quick look at Monroe himself. She was a straight-up bombshell and definitely a fish out of water out here. Even though this convoy was on a routine resupply mission to Camp Bastion—*it wasn't like they were going on a raid or anything*—every trip outside the wire was dangerous. Every mission required security and explosive-ordinance personnel to locate, detonate, or dispose of the mines. Every day, Marines lost their lives and limbs, and this girl seemed determined to be one of them. Just so she could take some stupid pictures, ask a few questions, write a stupid story. He didn't get it.

It hadn't been his idea to take her. He thought Lance Corporal Ryan did just fine, but the lieutenant had said she would be on some of the missions from now on, and he didn't question orders — ever. But he had told her right off the bat to leave that fruity-smelling shit in the tent. He didn't want any of that girly crap around his Marines. His platoon didn't spend much time around females unless they were in garrison, and at the moment, she was the only one for miles. At least she wasn't like some of the female Marines who went around all painted with makeup like they were looking for a date in the desert. They had no business acting like that in a combat zone. Women were enough of a distraction to the mission without fueling his troops' sex drives.

Geez, the MRAP was slow... he had been to Iraq in '03, '04, and again in '06. So he knew how vulnerable troops had been riding around in Humvees. He remembered early in the war when they had issued armored doors and body-length armored mats for the seats. They had helped with the blasts but not much. When Marines survived, they usually lost one or more body parts. Then the next generation of Humvees were so armored up that the armor weighted the vehicles down and caused mechanical failures. Parts would just break for the hell of it.

So now, Marines rode around in the MRAP — mine-resistant-ambush-protected — vehicles, which made for a painfully slow trip, mostly because of the minesweepers, but their efforts were helping Marines survive the improvised explosive devices. If they needed more speed, they used the M-ATVs, which were pretty well armored but light and fast like a Humvee, so they could still be taken out by the bigger daisy-chained bombs the insurgents had begun using to create incredible explosions. Marines were still giving up body parts on the regular.

He was glad they were in an MRAP, but he never felt safe. Not out here. And not even at home anymore. Hell, the desert seemed more like home than Houston did these days. He didn't know how to connect with civilians anymore, with their self-centered, self-righteous outlook on life, as if they were entitled to everything and had to work for nothing. *Responsibility, honor, self-sacrifice, respect* — they were just old-fashioned words to some people. To him, they were the essence of life.

So he had continuously volunteered for deployments, but he couldn't believe he had made it this long with all his digits. He had his cage rattled pretty good a few times — his brain had taken too many hits against his skull — and he had been required to spend a little extra time in garrison because of it. But he didn't understand how he had been so lucky for so long. He had buddies who had been killed on their first tours. He had a couple of friends who had returned to combat sporting prosthetics. He had another friend lose his leg in a motorcycle accident right after a seven-month pump to Iraq. He didn't know much about fate or destiny, but some things just seemed like bad luck to him.

He shook his head, took another look at the terrain, and then checked his watch. "We should be back in about thirty minutes," he said to his driver.

Monroe was back there chatting it up with Carter.

"Thanks for explaining about the baby powder. I'd been wondering what that was all about," she said.

"Well, if you're going to patrol with us, you need to know where to walk so you don't get blown up, don't you?" Carter said.

Hicks felt every kind thought he had of Monroe shrivel in a heartbeat. "First of all, Corporal Monroe will *not* be joining us on foot patrols. And second—*do not print that, Monroe!*" Sergeant Hicks hollered. "That's the problem with the media. For some reason, they think operational issues belong in the news. Next thing you know, we'll have insurgents sneaking around our roving patrols powdering false paths right over the mines. And get your eyes and rifle where they belong, Carter!"

Carter immediately raised his M-4 to point toward his sector and turned his eyes toward potential targets.

Monroe was sitting directly behind him, so he turned and leaned around his seat to be sure that she understood his meaning. But instead of her face, he saw the camera lens; heard a click; and then he felt, as much as heard, a deafening explosion.

Role-Play

Molly Monroe

Molly stared at her reflection, wondering what about her features was so remarkable that she should receive so much attention. She stared into her eyes, trying to see into her soul. Who was Molly Monroe? What purpose did she serve? Would she ever do anything that mattered? Would anyone ever see anything in her beyond her image?

She was only sixteen, but she had spent so much time in front of a camera, she could do still shots in her sleep. She knew the angles photographers preferred, and she could amuse herself indefinitely during the long sessions, listening to instructions on where to stand or sit, and silently playing characters that fit her mood. Modeling was just another performance.

Today she would pretend to be as alluring as Cleopatra. Molly thought Cleopatra had never felt awkward. If she could become the seductress queen of Egypt, she would be strong; she would be sensual – she would be powerful. Her life would mean something.

She stiffened her spine and slipped into character.

Nick Monroe

They hadn't made the announcement yet, but he turned off his cell phone anyway. He hadn't been able to check his messages because his ma was being nosy. But he knew Beth had texted him at least three times since he'd told her what he'd known about Molly's condition. He was probably being a jerk, but he couldn't help it. He needed to keep it together for his mom's sake and for Molly's.

Besides, in no small part, Molly's situation could easily be considered Beth's fault—and his, if he got right down to it.

"You don't want to hang around our high-school crowd tonight," Beth said. "We're just having one last sha-bang with our coffeehouse crew," and he knew she was referring to her thespian friends. Nick swore they were the most serious people on the planet. They didn't know how to have fun unless they were reciting a comedy.

"Well, John and I are having drinks downtown with some of his Marine buddies. So you two come find us after. We'll crash at the Marriott, okay?"

"You got it, babe." And Beth kissed him good-bye.

That was just before she had introduced Molly to scumbags who wouldn't know Tennessee Williams from Johnny Walker. Beth had lied to his face, and Molly had suffered greatly for it. Nick had not been able to forgive Beth. Too bad he hadn't been able to convince himself to stop loving her.

And then there was John. His parents were supposed to catch a flight to Germany tonight. Nick wasn't ready to deal with that grim reality yet. He felt like a vise-grip had a hold on his chest. Too much had happened in the last five days for him to process it all at once.

"Flight attendants, prepare for takeoff."

He watched the receding buildings of the Tampa International Airport lose size and shape as the plane picked up speed on the runway and propelled itself into the open air. He felt like he was caught in the jet wash, being tossed around between present and past, and feeling little hope for the future.

As if sensing his thoughts, his mother grabbed hold of his hand and squeezed until the plane was horizontal again.

Donna Monroe

She absolutely hated flying. Maybe it was because she knew there were many things a human body could do, and flying was not one of them. Maybe it was the complete and utter lack of control she had in an airplane. Maybe it was because angry people liked to shoot planes down—or highjack them. Whatever her reasons, any flight she had attempted without her medicine had made her feel extremely ill. She simply didn't respond well to flying. So maybe it was something as simple as air sickness. But she doubted it.

She had flown with Molly for a Miss Teen USA pageant, and the flight had been the only negative part of her trip. Oh, it wasn't terrible really. It was just that she lost interest in talking when she was on the prescription. So naturally, she had closed her eyes and listened to the contestants sitting around her.

"Miranda will be a contender, don't you think?"

"Are you kidding me? Have you seen her cankles? Those calves of hers sink right into her feet."

"I can't believe I didn't notice that, but you've seen how Trisha slumps when she walks? She looks like a camel."

"Really, there's no need to go through them one-by-one. There are only a couple from the East Coast who even stand a chance."

"I bet she will be at least a finalist."

"Who?"

"Molly Monroe."

"Yeah. She's got the face and body. But have you ever tried to talk to her? Not much on social skills. Her head's always in a book. Look at her. No telling how she'll respond when the judges ask her questions."

And that's when Donna had stopped listening. She had glanced over at Molly; of course she was reading. But Donna already knew how well Molly would perform when she had to answer questions. She had been drilling her with every question imaginable since she was five years old. Molly had the question-and-answer sessions down to a script.

Basic Warrior Stance

Recruit Molly Monroe

"The basic warrior stance is the foundation of all movements in the Marine Corps Martial Arts Program. Do you understand, recruits?"

"Yes, sir!"

"Hands closed, not clenched! Elbows in! Chin tucked! Good to go?"

"Yes, sir!"

"Feet shoulder-width apart! Knees slightly bent! Relaxed, not rigid! Good to go?"

"Yes, sir!"

"You must be relaxed but strong! Good to go?"

"Yes, sir!"

"Assume the basic warrior stance. Move!"

At every command, the recruits responded, "Marine Corps!" and executed the move.

"You will execute the lead-hand punch, understand?

"Yes, sir!"

"You throw the punch; you move; you execute. Good to go?"

"Yes, sir!"

"Lead hand punch!"

"Marine Corps!"

The whistle blew. Lead hand punch. Basic warrior stance. Whistle, lead-hand punch, basic warrior stance. Whistle, lead-hand punch, basic warrior stance. Whistle, lead-hand punch, basic warrior stance. Whistle, lead-hand punch, basic warrior stance. Whistle, lead-hand punch, basic warrior stance. Whistle, lead-hand punch, basic warrior stance. Whistle, whistle; freeze.

"Now that's how it's supposed to look right there, recruits. You don't just practice the move, you perfect it! Good to go?"

"Yes, sir!"

"Rear-hand punch! Move!"

"Marine Corps!"

The whistle blew. Rear-hand punch. Basic warrior stance. Whistle, rear-hand punch, basic warrior stance. Whistle, rear-hand punch, basic warrior stance. Whistle, rear-hand punch, basic warrior stance. Whistle, rear-hand punch, basic warrior stance. Whistle, rear-hand punch, basic warrior stance. Whistle, rear-hand punch, basic warrior stance. Whistle, whistle; freeze.

"After a while you'll learn a lot more strikes — where if your opponent throws a rear-hand punch, you can counter, understand?"

"Yes, sir!"

His name was Gunnery Sergeant Simmons, but she secretly called him Othello. He was even fiercer, more intimidating than the other drill instructors. His face was etched of ebony, and his eyes were the gray of river rock; his limbs were as tawny and strong as a great oak. He wore a black belt with his utility trousers, and his black T-shirt read, "One mind, any weapon." He had spoken of the "ethical warrior" before he began teaching them how to kill.

"Uppercut!"

"Marine Corps!"

The whistle blew. Uppercut. Basic warrior stance. Whistle, uppercut, basic warrior stance. Whistle, uppercut, basic warrior stance. Whistle, uppercut, basic warrior stance. Whistle, uppercut, basic warrior stance. Whistle uppercut, *basic warrior stance. Whistle, uppercut, basic warrior stance. Whistle, whistle; freeze.*

She had done the math. She knew what she had to do to be like him. Twenty-seven point five training hours for a tan belt; twenty-nine more for gray. Thirty more for green; thirty-five more for brown. Thirty-four point five more for black belt first degree, and seventy total sustainment hours between the levels. She would have to pass a test for every belt.

"Right hook! Move!"

"Marine Corps!"

The whistle blew. Right hook. Basic warrior stance. Whistle, right hook, basic warrior stance. Whistle, right hook, basic warrior stance. Whistle, right hook, basic warrior stance. Whistle, right hook, basic warrior stance. Whistle, right hook, basic warrior stance. Whistle, right hook, basic warrior stance. Whistle, whistle; freeze.

She executed every move with precision. Punch. Strike. Choke. Again. Strike. Execute. Move. Again. Fall. Kick. Throw. Again. Knife techniques. Pugil sticks. Again and again. Weapons of opportunity. Strike! Unarmed restraints. Move! Armed manipulations. Execute!

Never be a victim again.

"Left hook! Move!"

"Marine Corps!"

The whistle blew. Left hook. Basic warrior stance. Whistle, left hook, basic warrior stance. Whistle, left hook, basic warrior stance. Whistle, left hook, basic warrior stance. Whistle, left hook, basic warrior stance. Whistle, left hook, basic warrior stance. Whistle, left hook, basic, warrior stance. Whistle, whistle; freeze.

Never be a victim again!

Sergeant Andrew Hicks

Sergeant Hicks knew that when shit hit the fan, there really wasn't time to think—just to act. The whole point of Marine Corps training was to teach the body muscle memory. So when he felt the explosion so close to his position, he knew without anyone having to tell him that his supply-convoy mission had just been altered, and he would have to take charge.

He turned his attention to the front of the convoy in time to see a falling Osprey, on fire, with a giant hole like a cracked nut in the center, land on its side about five hundred meters to the north of his lead vehicle. The right rudder shattered, and its rotors dispersed like giant spinning knives around the crash site. He didn't think the bird would explode—it wasn't a Cobra, those babies were nothing but weapons and fuel, and he had seen one of them light up a dark night in Iraq—but he knew intuitively that he had to form a hasty security perimeter, put the fire out, prepare for ambush, and provide a med assist as needed. They would defend the Marines and equipment until the fire support and recovery teams arrived.

It took him less than sixty seconds to make the assessment and begin barking orders.

First Lieutenant John Michaelson

As soon as John heard the explosion, he knew it wasn't far from the camp. He fastened his Kevlar helmet on his head as he ran toward the Combat Operations Center. Sergeant Stinson caught up with him on his way.

"It was an Osprey, sir. Attacked with rocket-propelled grenades."

"What the hell? I thought those birds could withstand an RPG attack. Do we have the battle-damage assessment yet?"

"No, sir, but Corporal Dye found them with the video feed, and it looks like one of the Ospreys crashed nearly on top of Sergeant Hick's convoy. The other bird made it back to base but had to make an emergency landing. They've launched a Harrier and the Cobras for air support."

"Has the Quick Reaction Force responded?"

"Yes, sir."

"ETA?"

"About ten minutes, sir."

"Was the convoy ambushed?"

"I don't know, sir. I left as quickly as I could to find you."

His heart was racing as they entered the tent. It was buzzing with activity. Several Marines were huddled around the video feed. Others were typing hectically, to give and receive information in the secured chat rooms, and the radios were squawking with situation reports. As soon as he looked at the video screen, he saw that the convoy had formed a hasty security perimeter around the downed helicopter and were receiving and returning fire. Then he saw the Cobras on the screen; when they launched the hellfire missiles and began taking out the insurgents on mopeds, the Marines shouted various cheers of approval—"Yut,

yut! Get those hajji bastards! Oorah!" —before returning to their reporting procedures.

He sat down at a chat terminal to assess the level of effort from his higher headquarters and the other units in the area of operations. Since the Quick Reaction Force was engaged, the camp headquarters element would be participating in this skirmish too. But all the words on his computer screen were blurring together. He was struggling to concentrate on his duties.

He looked back at the video feed. Molly was in the middle of that mess, and there wasn't a thing he could do but trust Sergeant Hicks to bring her back alive.

Lance Corporal Vanessa Ramirez

The thunderous noise seemed to suck the laughter out of the female tent in one swift blast. Gossip and games ceased, and their training took over. Ramirez began relacing her boots and putting her uniform back on. Some of the others were taking roll, according to section, so the senior members of each unit would have the information required to report to their platoon sergeants. Ramirez had to get to the Mortuary Affairs hut, not only for accountability but also because attacks usually meant casualties. And casualties meant she would have to process remains. Vanessa was genuinely scared. Her job was hard enough to handle most of the time. But she had a gut feeling that her best friend was involved in whatever was happening outside the wire, and she couldn't think about that right now.

Fireworks

Molly Monroe

Nick had left her alone with John often enough for her to think that he had been trying to set them up. Not that she needed any help in that area. There were plenty of guys at school interested in her, although most of them were boring jocks without an iota of intellect. But John was different. Oh, he was handsome, but everything about him was easy and fresh, all the way down to his soapy scent. She was certain he didn't ever wear cologne, and she interpreted that to mean that he wasn't trying to get down her pants. And she loved talking and listening to him. He could switch conversations from football, to literature, to politics, to mechanics without thinking twice about it. Not that she knew anything about anything except liberal arts, but he could make any subject interesting – especially when he talked about the Marine Corps. He couldn't wait to be commissioned, and he was in such a hurry that he had taken classes during the summers and would be graduating college early. His enthusiasm and determination inspired her. He was captivating.

She realized she looked forward to his visits more lately. Even though he and Nick had been friends all through college, she hadn't paid much attention to him until recently. When Nick and Beth became a couple and they had begun making plans as a foursome, she felt awkward and was reluctant. Now she looked forward to their frequent outings.

John actually listened to her. She couldn't believe it at first; she was about to be a senior in high school, and he was on the cusp of finishing college. Yet he never treated her like a kid three years younger.

They had spent the day at Tiger Stadium. Nick had suggested that the four of them go there to see the Fourth of July fireworks display. They had to get there early to get a good spot, and they had camped out for hours during the day, lying on blankets, eating sandwiches and chips, and washing it all down with coke and beer.

By the time the fireworks show began, she knew she wanted John to kiss her. But she knew better than to show it. He wouldn't want an easy girl. He would want a girl he could respect, and she knew how to be that girl. Her mother had taught her how. She was lying on the blanket, watching the colors explode above her, inhaling the soapy, grassy, gunpowder scents. When he leaned into her field of vision and kissed her – at that moment – it was the best experience of her life.

Nick Monroe

"Jack and coke, please." He ignored the disapproving glance his ma gave him, and that humming thing she did when she was agitated. When the flight attendant moved on, he said, "We all have our vices, Ma, so quit judging me already."

She whispered, obviously embarrassed, "It's not even noon yet, Nicky."

He rolled his eyes and said, "It's five o'clock somewhere."

She studied her crossword puzzle as if it held life's treasures and hummed a little louder, making him regret speaking up, even if he had meant it.

This is how she was with everything she disapproved. She would drive you crazy until you did what she wanted you to do. Most of the time, it was easier to either do what she expected, or let her think you were meeting her expectations. He couldn't remember ever having had a drink in front of her before.

He usually only let her in on the things he knew she could handle. He was a math teacher, he coached the football team, and he lived in Tampa. These were all areas of his life that made her happy. He dated on occasion and would joke with her about his failed attempts at love, and she would praise him for trying and encourage him to continue—like any good mother would. But it all seemed like a game to him. He catered to her ideas on family so she could exist peacefully in her world of make-believe. He had no intention of confiding how he had spent so many of his weekends or his desire to join the police force. Anything outside of her bubbly world was omitted from conversation.

He had watched her fall apart after his dad died, and though only seven years old at the time, he had known that he was the man of the house and that it was his job to protect the women. So he had fallen into the habit of taking care of Molly and keeping anything that would upset his mom from her. He had been the one to clean Molly's messes when the bed wetting started: her bed, her sheets, and her clothes. He had been the one to chase away Molly's nightmares. Nick had become the father. He patched Molly up when she was hurt, and he chased away all her *wannabe* boyfriends.

And then he got so distracted with Beth, he practically threw Molly into John's arms. He thought John would think of her as a kid sister too. He thought he would protect her when Nick wasn't watching. Instead, they had become an item right in front of him. And it had been hard for him to swallow at first.

"What the hell are you doing, John?"

"What? The same thing you're doing, bro."

Nick grabbed him, pulled him away from Molly, and said, "She's too young for you! You're supposed to be watching her, not…"

"She's the same age as Beth. It doesn't seem to be a problem for you!"

They were in each other's faces screaming, and Nick was making his point, "But she's my kid sister! She – "

Then Molly stood between them and interrupted him, "Hey!"

"What?" Nick hollered.

"Don't I get a say in the matter, Nicky?"

And that had been all it took. She had cocked her head and pleaded with her baby blues. He had realized that she had chosen John, and Nick liked to think he let her make her own choices. Besides, he knew John would treat her right, and he could keep an eye on them. She had given him a hard time later for ruining her first kiss, which had also shocked and elated him. He had secretly patted himself on the back for keeping the wolves at bay for so long—it made him feel better about throwing her at John. He figured they would be a dead-end from the beginning. John was going to be a Marine, and Molly was going off to college in North Carolina. But in the meantime, John would protect her.

And he did. Until the night they all let her down.

He swallowed the last of his drink and hit the service button.

"Can I get you anything, sir?"

"Yeah. Another Jack and coke, please." He totally tuned out his ma's humming.

Crucible

Recruit Molly Monroe

Staff Sergeant Martinez reminded them, "Pain is weakness leaving the body. So embrace it, recruits!"

Fifty-four hours with eight for sleeping and three meals to eat. Thirty-six stations; twenty-nine problem-solving exercises. Forty-eight miles with forty-five pounds, plus rifle, helmet, flak. Bloody blisters in suede boots. Sand fleas dining on skin sopping with grime and sweat. Up and over every obstacle; crawling through wet earth, under concertine wire; continuing forward; ignoring pain, fatigue, and fear as explosions enveloped them. Swamp stench blending with gun powder. The body does what the mind wills it to do.

She knew how to leave her body, to let it follow commands even as her mind dreamt of faraway places, lost friends, and lost loves. Her ears were tuned in to the instructors while her heart held a dialogue with her past. Sometimes she even imagined herself marching with the Bard — begging for a sonnet, an insult, a joke — any pithy quote to get her through the moment. She treasured his wit, and she tried to return it. They made new conversations with his centuries-old wisdom. She had been told she had a new family now — "we few, we happy few, we band of brothers" — but he was her only friend on this lonely island. He knew her as well as she knew herself. "He jests at scars that never felt a wound," he'd say. "So true," she would reply. "If all else fail, myself have power to die."

"Squad, halt!"

But there would be times when she would need her mind. Her body would be unable to simply obey as it had for most humps. She — they all — would have to think their way through much of the crucible. They were separated into squads, as the warrior stations had been designed for team building. No one could complete these obstacles alone.

The obstacles were all named after Medal of Honor recipients except for one. "Corporal Laville's Duty" was named for a female Marine who had given her life helping others escape from a fire in 1944. They stood in front of the complex obstacle of six cable-suspended tires, positioned seven feet apart, and they listened as Sergeant Lane gave the instructions:

"Your squad has secured the top floor of a building. It has caught fire, and the only way out is over those cables to the neighboring building. The cables are suspended between the two buildings, and your mission is to get your squad and equipment to the safety of the other building. Only one team member can be on a tire at a time, and if any Marine or gear touches the deck, they will be eliminated from the problem.

"The fire will consume the first building in twenty-five minutes.

"Recruit Monroe, you'll be the team leader for this station. Are there any questions?"

First Lieutenant John Michaelson

John hadn't been able to take his eyes off the video feed. One of the Osprey's pilots had reported casualties shortly after the crash, but his transmission had been garbled, and he was believed to have been semiconscious. And there hadn't been any communications with the bird since then. They hadn't observed any convoy casualties, but it wasn't always clear what was happening on the ground from where he sat inside the Combat Operations Center, usually called the COC. He suspected there would be more killed and wounded before this whole thing was over, and he couldn't shake his growing anxiety over who could be among them. And although he hoped for a quick response to the crash, the insurgents kept coming up with creative and deadly ways of expanding their initial attacks by setting traps for first responders and recovery teams, so rescues were tricky. He wished he was out there himself because it would give him some sense of control over the situation. There was little to do in the COC except "assess and report," but you couldn't trust reports while shots were still being fired; he knew firsthand how the fog of war could interfere with accurate reporting.

Even in the Combat Operations Center, all the activity could get confusing—and this was truer than ever for him now. He had brain fog of another sort and a storm in his gut to boot.

He focused on being calm. He tried to apply the same rational thought to this situation as he had in previous skirmishes. In the moments between giving and receiving information, he thought about what was going on in the downed Osprey. The AirBoss had passed that it was unlikely the bird would explode, so he hoped Molly was inside. Of course, it would be a terrible place to be if the insurgents were equipped to attack it with rockets or mortars again; it was more than likely that the flares equipped on the Osprey to deflect incoming missiles were damaged during the crash. He hoped they would receive some good intelligence soon.

He had tried to figure out what had happened to the Osprey. He was interested in the fact that it had landed on its side and not upside down as he had heard about in the test flights. He wondered how fast it had been going when it hit the ground. It didn't look too damaged, except for the right side. The whole right wing was missing.

He was still watching the video feed when the screen went dark and the thermal images blurred into green fuzz.

"Sir, the Cobras are in brown-out conditions, and the Quick Reaction Force has slowed to a snail's pace. This sandstorm just rolled in out of nowhere. They've decided to send in another Osprey with the back-up Quick Reaction team. Estimated departure in five minutes."

Sergeant Andrew Hicks

He was pretty sure their radio communications hadn't been good. But they'd needed every trigger-puller during the attack, and now that the sandstorm had given them a lull in the fighting, he could reassess the situation and report it.

He radioed commands to the convoy to remain in their defensive posture, directed Carter to determine the battle-damage assessment of the perimeter, and let the team know that he would assess the bird and crew. Then he entered the Osprey through the open tail end and immediately noticed that the .50-cal. machine gun wasn't mounted to the ramp. He had been aware of the weapon intersecting with his field of fire during the firefight, but he hadn't made the connection that the "Ma-Deuce" machine gun had been retrieved from the aircraft. But he should have. He should have paid closer attention. Even as he thought about it now, he realized he couldn't remember a face behind the weapon. He wondered if it was the Osprey's gunner. He thought the Marine might still be in position, taking a beating by the sandstorm with the rest of them. He made a mental note to confirm or disprove his suspicions and account for that Marine in his report to higher headquarters.

His first order after the crash had been to send Hart and Monroe, the newbie and the girl, inside the bird to provide medical assistance to the crew and passengers. Their own corpsman, Petty Officer Galloway, had been in the rear vehicle and the farthest from the crash site when the shit went down, and he had decided to leave the Doc at his weapon until it was safe for him to move from his position.

The sand pelted the metal exterior of the cabin, and the wind roared through the openings. The storm made it dark in the bird, so he looked toward the cockpit and waited for his eyes to adjust. As far as he could tell, the right side of the cabin was jagged and torn, and he could see daypacks and personal supplies in heaps. He could tell by the gear and equipment that several Marines must have been, or still were, on board, but this scene didn't look good as far as survivability was concerned. His eyes began dilating around the same time his nose caught the stench of burned flesh and excrement penetrating the metallic odor of gunpowder, and he recognized the sights and smells of human carnage.

He almost shit his pants when he saw Monroe. She was covered in blood, and her face was white. She had white powder in her hair and on her cammies. She looked like a ghost. She was mumbling something, and he didn't have a freakin' clue what she was trying to tell him.

"...many times before their deaths. The valiant never taste death but once."

"What the hell, Monroe? Where's Hart?" She looked like she was about to go belly up on him, so he knew he couldn't go easy on her. "Give me the casualty report, Corporal."

"Sixteen KIA. One MIA. One WIA."

"Okay. Sixteen dead; one missing...what's the status on the wounded Marine?"

"An urgent surgical. Shredded legs. I applied tourniquets and morphine, but he's gonna need Doc Galloway soon. One of the killed in action was alive when I got here, Sergeant. He died in my arms."

Her voice was unsteady, and he could tell she had the shakes. He knew it was a normal human reaction, especially for a POG—person other than a grunt—on the first run-in with death, but they didn't have time for that emotional crap out here. He had too many questions—where she'd gotten the morphine, for example. But he needed the essentials first, and he had to keep her focused before she turned into a blubbering baby. "An MIA? Are you sure, Monroe? And where the hell is Hart?"

"Hart dismounted the fifty-cal. machine gun and took charge of a sector."

"Roger that. So who's missing?"

"The Marine who…his name was Jones…"

He dug in his cargo pocket for a pen. "Roger. The missing Marine is Jones. Do you know his rank?"

"No. Jones told me about the MIA. He was screaming before he died. A huge chunk of the helicopter was stuck in his stomach. And his body was…"

"The MIA, Monroe!" he yelled at her now. There was nothing they could do about the dead Marine, but if one was missing, the insurgents could get their raggedy-ass hands on him, torture him, and eventually behead him. "Tell me about the missing Marine right this minute, Monroe!"

"It's the gunner, Sergeant. He fell out of the back after they were hit, before the crash."

Private First Class Dakota Hart

He couldn't see anything, but he stayed at the ready with the Ma-Deuce machine gun, and he let the sand scrape his face dry. He didn't know whether to be proud or ashamed of himself, and he didn't know if Sergeant Hicks was going to pat him on the back or kick him in the ass, but he knew whichever it was, it would be in front of the whole squad, so he decided to get ready for an ass-whooping. He'd take it like a man.

Whatever he had coming, it would be a hell of a lot easier than walking into that stinking death pit had been. He had tried to help Corporal Monroe. She had stormed into the Osprey on a mission, checking pulses and screaming over the gunfire, looking for survivors. He had started out all right. He had seen smoke up front and, convinced the bird was going to explode, had grabbed a fire extinguisher and sprayed the damn thing dry. He hadn't realized he'd sprayed her too until he heard her screaming at him to stop. Then he saw what she was doing. She was kneeling next to a Marine and holding his head in her lap. The Marine was screaming too, but he wasn't saying anything comprehensible. He had a huge chunk of metal pinning him to the floor of the bird that left his guts exposed. His legs were mangled. Hart looked the Marine in the eyes and realized that under the pain and fear etched in the lines of his face was knowledge. The Marine knew he was going to die.

"Hart! Listen to me!"

He hadn't realized she had been speaking to him. His ears were ringing from all the noise.

"You've got to dig through these packs and find a medical kit. Not one of our combat-life-saver kits. One of these guys must have been a corpsman."

He had nodded and started looking.

"ASAP, Hart! And let me know if you see any more WIA."

He had made eye contact so that she would know he'd heard her. But he felt too jacked up to speak at that point. He'd found the kit and another live Marine at the same time. He'd checked him, found a pulse, grabbed the kit, and tried not to step on bodies as he headed back to Corporal Monroe.

He had handed her the kit and said, "We've got another live one, Corporal."

She had taken the kit from him and dug through it in a hurry, all the while talking to the Marine like he was her best friend; then she kissed him on the forehead and emptied a preloaded needle into his arm. The Marine quit screaming, and Hart realized she had given him morphine. She had kept talking, but it didn't seem like she was talking to anyone in particular. She held the Marine, slightly rocking back and forth, and she said, "O proud death, what feast is toward in thine eternal cell, that thou so many princes at a shot so bloodily hast struck."

Hart was still trying to figure out if she was praying or losing her mind when she stood up and said, "Where's the other one?"

He had pointed and followed her.

The lower half of the second WIA's body was covered with gear and equipment: tactical radios, mostly. His legs were goners too. And the Marine had defecated on himself. It was too much for Hart.

"Corporal, they need me out there!" he'd screamed. He had hoped she'd believed him. He'd hoped she thought the sergeant had called him on the radio. He prayed she hadn't seen him hurl his beef stew over the ramp before dismounting the .50 cal. He had hoped she thought he was brave.

It had felt damn good to fire the Ma-Deuce at those hajjis. He had wanted to kill them all for what they had done to his brothers. He didn't have to know those Marines to mourn them or avenge them. They were his family.

As the sandstorm ravaged his face, he held his weapon at the ready, hoping for another chance.

Mise en Abyme

Molly Monroe

It had been her idea, her design, her choreography. And Molly could think of no other place she would rather be. The music of Michael Mikulin filled the stage as they glided to his composition of "Blow, Blow, Thou Winter Wind." The lights were dimmed in the auditorium, and the spotlights were on Beth and her dancing in perfect harmony, mirror images of each other performing pirouettes, sautés, sissonnes, and tours – completing the ballet with a tour de force. She loved the irony in juxtapositions. A patchwork of art. Ballet and Shakespeare. Beth and Molly.

> *And when the music ended, the narrator said,*
> *"All the world's a stage,*
> *And all the men and women merely players;*
> *They have their exits and entrances,*
> *And one man in his time plays many parts,*
> *His acts being seven ages…"*

And all the dancers entered. Those dressed as infants; then schoolboys; then lovers and soldiers, politicians, and wrinkly, silver-haired merchants until finally, the solitary crippled old man entered stage right and exited stage left – diapered and demented, crawling to his dirt-strewn cradle.

Then the dancers became the chorus – to an a capella rendition of "Sonnet 62" – and Beth and Molly were mirror images once again, facing each other through the frame. Their movements were in unison – the mime and her reflection – until Molly turned her back on the looking glass.

Then Molly's reflection pulled her through the frame and took her place on center stage.

The mime and her reflection bowed proudly to a standing ovation.

Beth Bailey

"You have to help me!"

"Please calm down, ma'am. I do want to help. I just have to find someone who..."

"Oh my God, stop calling me ma'am! Beth. My name is Beth. And I am calm!"

"Okay, Beth. How about we go to my gunny's office?"

She hadn't realized she was screaming until the stillness of the office and his soft-spoken response reminded her of her surroundings. There were four other recruiters working in the main office, and one of them had a family at his desk (all of them staring at her). Two recruiters sat at their own desks watching her, with phones pressed against their ears, their hands covering their mouthpieces, and the other recruiter was walking toward her with a box of tissues in his hand. Now she was having a meltdown? In front of an audience, no less.

The other recruiter handed her the tissues, smiled, and walked away.

She dabbed at her eyes. "Okay," she said, in little more than a whisper. "What's your name?"

"Sergeant Jackson. But you can call me Jeff." He guided her toward a hallway and said, "My gunny may know how to help you. As I was saying, I'd love to, but I don't know your friend, and you haven't really given me anything to go on. I don't have access to 3270."

"Thirty-two what?"

"Thirty-two seventy is an administrative database the Corps uses. But that's not the point. The Corps's pretty small, and my gunny seems to know everybody in it. He'll be able to help." He directed her to a bench next to a closed office door. "I'll need to…"

A loud classical melody interrupted him.

Beth reached for her phone and said, "I'm sorry; I need to take this." She turned her back to him when she answered. "Hello." She didn't notice when Sergeant Jackson walked into the office without her, but she was already certain he would help her find Molly. "Please let my understudy take it. I may be gone awhile."

Confidence Course

Recruit Molly Monroe

Dirty name; run, jump, and swing. Stairway to heaven, inverted wall, cargo net, monkey bridge, slide for life, tough one, weaver, balancing logs, hand walk, wall climb, and skyscraper.

Fear is the only obstacle on the path to courage.

Stand on a log and jump to the next; it's not so far away. Don't worry that it's slick, and you could break your ribs or slide off and over and land on your head. It's only in your mind, you know. That's fear that you carry. Let it go; let it go. Don't think. Just move. Reach your potential, Monroe. Now, run and grab the rope, and swing to the other side. Keep your grip tight.

"That's rope burn, knucklehead! Next time you'll listen!"

Climb your way to the sky on the oversized ladder thirty feet high. Don't look down. Don't look down! Left foot. Up! Left foot. Up! Higher now. Climb over the top rung so you can go down. Quit shaking. You aren't allowed to cry! Move, legs, move.

"We don't have all stinkin' day, you nasty little worms! Move! Move! Move!"

A rush on the ground. Thankful to be alive. Run to the wall. It has no grooves, so jump and grab hold; strong arm or chicken wing. Use your muscles, scramble over, and go. Run to the cargo net – go, go, go!

"Hands on the vertical ropes; feet on horizontals. Get up my cargo net, recruit! Five, four, three, two, one! You're done!"

Monkey bridge, monkey bridge; not as high as the stairs. You can do this one, Monroe. Now go! Both hands on the top rope, both feet on the bottom. Slide across the ropes, hand to hand, foot to foot. Don't look down; you aren't afraid of heights. No fear, no fear, no fear. Marines never quit.

Slide for life; up, up, up the stairs. And down the rope headfirst. Lying prone on the rope. Ankles crossed over it. Knees dangling. Hand over hand and you pull yourself forward. Stop when you're halfway down. Let yourself fall so you are under the rope, holding on with your hands and ankles. Switch your direction so you are feet first. The rope wobbles; the water beckons. Ignore the whispers. Feet first now. Hand over hand. Going down. Toward the dry land. No fear. No fear. You've got this, Monroe.

The tough one's not so tough. It's just a rope. Climb the rope faster, even though you're tired. Climb to the platform. It's so high up. Oh no – it's going down that's hard. Grab the rope. It dangles there, just out of reach. Lean out to grab the rope, and then don't lose your grip! No fear, no fear. You can do this. Keep going, or you'll die. Cowardice is the worst kind of death.

"Why are you standing there, recruit? Move it now!"

Grab it and go. Down, down, down. Never slide down the rope!

"That's rope burn, genius! Next time, try following instructions!"

Run to the fifteen-foot A-frame. Lie on the log in the prone position. Weaver over the log, weaver under the log, all the way to the top. It's only fifteen feet high, so you can't stop. Half as high as the stairway to heaven; this is nothing. Go! Weaver over, weaver under till shoulders are tired and lungs out of breath. The monotony, unbearable. No matter. It will be *over soon. Then another run. And then balancing logs. Thankful for something easy. Cake walk to balance; they call this an obstacle?*

"Move it, recruit! Get on my hand walk! What's your problem, recruit? Didn't you have monkey bars on the playground when you were a child? Oh, let me guess; you were too busy on the PlayStation, weren't you? Go back to the beginning! You deprived child! You need more practice."

Run, run, run. Use the ropes to climb over the wall and down the other side. Go, go, go; never fast enough. Don't look up. Don't think about the skyscraper, the three-story building with no walls and slanted beams. Just climb. Climb till you reach the top, and then don't look down. This isn't really a skyscraper; it's just a pile of wood. Move one foot, and then the next. Down the cargo net. No fear. No fear. Marines never quit. Fear is the only obstacle.

Fear is the only obstacle!

"Five, four, three, two, one! You're done! Now form it up. We're moving out!"

Fear is the only obstacle!

"Pla – toon. Atten – tion! Uh – right…face! For – ward…march!"

"Well, you can have your Army khakis,
And you can have your Air Force blues,
'Cause there's a better breed of fighter
I'll introduce to you.
Their uniforms are different
Than any you've ever seen.
The Germans called them Devil Dogs;
Their title is Marine.
They were born at Parris Island,
The land that time forgot.
The sand was eighteen inches thick.
The sun was blazing hot…"

Lance Corporal Vanessa Ramirez

This was her first time outside the wire, and like a dumb ass, she had requested to go. She had never been assigned to collect body parts and personal effects from the scene. She had not planned on volunteering, and as the only female in the detachment, she assumed she would probably never be "voluntold" to go. Most of the time, when they treated her like a little sister they had to protect, she resented it. But during this deployment, she had secretly appreciated the gesture.

Ramirez was used to being one of the detachment members who waited at the hut in eerie silence, methodically preparing the simple wooden hut with four walls and no windows for the return of the team. She laid out goggles, scissors, collection bags, and pens. She placed the identification forms on clipboards and organized all the required gear beside each processing table. On days like today, when they expected more bodies than they had tables, she would prepare extra supplies to help with the transition from one body to the next. Each body would be respectfully prepared for its ceremonial transfer on its final voyage home.

When the team brought back the bodies, there was a set procedure. They worked as one as they identified and processed the remains of their fallen brothers and sisters. They had all learned their roles, and together they moved as a single entity. Ramirez always did the paperwork. One of the forms was used to provide basic information about the Marine, such as name, rank, social security number, and birth date. The other form had a diagram of the front and back of a human body. They used it to document identifying marks and lost limbs. Whenever body parts were missing, they had to be shaded black.

But this time was different. She had known as soon as she had walked into the hut that she couldn't think; she couldn't wait here not knowing what happened to Molly. She couldn't think about having to shade her black. So she had requested to go out with the collection team. And yeah, she was scared.

"Ramirez, do you remember everything they taught you in Twenty-Nine Palms?"

"Huh?" Ramirez snapped her head up when she realized her sergeant was speaking to her. "Um, sorry, Sergeant, say again?"

"Do you remember the procedures for isolating the area, marking the body parts, and sorting and organizing them and the personal effects?"

"Yes, Sergeant."

"Roger that. I still want you to stick with Corporal Stanley. He'll oversee your work, understood?"

"Yes, Sergeant."

"Good. Now keep your head in the game." He turned and shouted to the rest of the team, "ETA, five minutes. Prepare to suit up. The Quick Reaction Force has reported twenty-two casualties. This may take a while."

First Lieutenant John Michaelson

Movement in the Combat Operations Center had quieted since the Quick Reaction Force and Mortuary

Affairs had taken over the crash site. There were still incoming and outgoing reports to keep them all busy, but the enthusiasm of the hellfire missiles had been replaced by a forlorn undercurrent since the KIA and MIA reports had hit. Cobras provided air security on scene, but it appeared the insurgents had cleared the area. The Intelligence team and a few of the Special Ops guys had disappeared into a more secure facility to discuss and implement a classified plan for locating the missing gunner.

John was currently occupied by a report from the AirBoss. Apparently, they had decided to rescue the bird instead of destroying it, and since it was so close to the camp, they could do it relatively quickly. They wouldn't need to dispatch an overnight security element. They expected to recover the Osprey within the next few hours, and that was a good thing for him because the security element usually came from either his unit or the military police. This time around, the Quick Reaction Force would provide security until the Osprey was recovered.

Sergeant Stinson interrupted his train of thought. "Sir, Sergeant Hicks's convoy is back in the compound. He's confirmed they had no casualties. They're doing ammo counts and vehicle inspections, and then they're going to break for changeover and chow. Sergeant Hicks passed that debrief will go at nineteen thirty."

"Thank you, Sergeant Stinson. Notify Sergeant Hicks that I'll be there for the debriefing."

"Aye, sir."

Thank God his Marines had made it back alive—but especially Molly. He didn't know how he could live with himself if anything had happened to her. He hoped this run-in with death would deter her ambition to get out of the camp. And well, if it didn't, he would just have to figure something out.

He couldn't wait to see her at the debriefing. It was good knowing she was okay, but he really needed to see her for himself.

Sergeant Brian Price

He had been waiting for more than an hour. When Alpha Company had finally bothered to tell him what was going on with Monroe, he had driven to their compound to wait with them for word on the convoy. He had been stunned when he saw her. She looked worse than the rest of them. All the others were speckled with sand and smelled like gunpowder, but only she and one other scrawny, wide-eyed PFC had blood on their uniforms. He waited for her to turn in her ammo and then even longer so Sergeant Hicks could speak with her alone.

He tried to keep his face neutral when she walked over to their Humvee. She looked like a different person, and he hoped he wasn't gawking. It was like she was in slow motion, almost tip-toeing, walking on water and watching every step. Her hair had loosened from its tight braid and was falling in strands around her face. Her lips wore a pout that needed lifting, and her eyes were glossy. She looked like she needed someone, and in that moment, he wished she needed him. He wanted to comfort her.

But he'd be damned if he was going to let her see him going soft on her again. He leaned against the front tire and resisted the urge to open the passenger door for her. Monroe would bite his head off at any attempt at chivalry.

"Thanks for coming to get me, Sergeant Price."

"No problem. I heard you had a hell of a day. Thought you might need a lift." He was surprised and grateful when she smiled at him.

She got in the Humvee, and he let the silence linger for a few minutes. But he had been standing around too long, too worried, to wait any longer to hear her voice.

"I was worried sick when I heard what happened."

"I'm fine, Sergeant," she said.

"It's just us in the vehicle, Molly. No need to 'sergeant' me. Remember?"

"Yes." She looked at herself in the mirror and inspected her hands and uniform as if she was just noticing her appearance.

He said, "You might feel fine, but you could be in shock. We should go by medical. You're covered in blood."

"It's not mine."

"But I think you should get checked out."

"I just want to get back so I can take a shower."

Good God. He didn't want to talk about a shower. "That's gotta suck. Wearing someone else's blood on your uniform. Are you okay?"

"I said I'm fine."

"You don't look fine," he said.

Her silence was frustrating. Sometimes she talked to him like they were best friends, and then other times she completely shut him out.

"I wish you would talk to me," he said.

"Okay, well. I'll have the story ready tonight. And the pictures will be amazing. I got a shot of the Osprey going down."

"That's great. I mean that you got some good pictures. Not that the Osprey went down. I was really more concerned about you. Your well-being."

"Really? I think that's just what you tell yourself," she said.

"What are you talking about, Molly? I'm pretty sure I've always been there for you, whether you realize it or not. Even if we had not become friends, Marines take care of their own."

"I think all you really want is to rub it in that you warned me that it sucks out there!"

"Why in the hell would you say that? I've done no such thing!"

"Or maybe you're just trying to get down my pants again!"

"That's a low blow and completely unfair, and you know it, Molly."

"It's Monroe. You can let me out here, Sergeant."

"But we're not even close…"

"Please let me out, Sergeant Price! I'll walk from here!"

Damn, she had become unpredictable. He had no idea why she was pitching a fit, but he didn't want to make it worse. So he pulled over and had just enough time to fully brake before she jumped out and slammed the door.

What the hell? He sat alone in the Humvee and watched her walk away until her desert digital uniform blended in with the sand-packed road.

Phantoms

Molly Monroe

Music boomed, pulsed, peaked. Colors blasted pink, orange, and green. White strobes flashed; bodies twisted, rolled, throbbed, and tweaked. Rainbows and fireflies, shadows and skin, smoke and cologne, mulberry incense. She was light and hot and wet with sweat. But nothing mattered. She was free and moving, dancing and loving — beautiful like a butterfly.

A sea of bodies, floating phantoms, drifters in a coral reef. An undercurrent pushing her toward the warm, dark Amazon. Swimming and swaying; swirling in eddies and buddies and griffins. A boa on her back and lava in her veins.

A phantom whispered, "The underground is bigger than the surface, baby; you belong to me now."

And she was lifted. Cradled. Thirsty: she sipped from salty skin and felt a rumble of laughter against her lips.

Echoes. Cavernous whispers. Phantoms.

And she fell into the empty night.

And crashed on a cold slab of rock.

Slashed garments. Searing skin. Pain outside and in.

Buddies, eddies, and griffins.

Donna Monroe

She wedged the blanket the flight attendant had given her between their seats and eased Nick's head against it. She did not approve of his drinking, but at least he could sleep now.

Her body had responded to the prescription, which seemed to have taken the edge off more than just her fear of flying. Thankfully, she didn't feel like she was suffocating anymore. But her mind had not relaxed in the least. Her thoughts ran in an endless stream. Long-forgotten memories resurfaced. She supposed it took effort to forget, and all her efforts were focused on *hope* right now: hope that Molly would survive. Hope that Molly would forgive her. Hope that Molly would leave the Marines. And though she tried not to acknowledge it, she sensed another hope lingering beneath the surface: the hope that Molly would still be beautiful.

If she were honest with herself, she would admit that was really bothering her. Donna had always seen so much potential in Molly. She had such gentleness and beauty that everyone who knew her adored her. Donna had believed that Molly was the kind of girl people would listen to and follow. But the thought never would have crossed her mind that Molly would join the military. And of all services, the Marines—the most ruthless of them all, *for crying out loud!*

She wondered what Matthew would have thought about *this*. He may have considered Molly's wounds to be an unfortunate but necessary price of freedom and an honorable sacrifice. He had been quite the patriot. Not that she wasn't—she just believed that there were other ways to represent one's country. There were other means of servitude more appropriate for ladies than carrying guns, fighting like a man, and going off to war.

She imagined Matthew would have been as proud as a peacock when Molly joined, pleased that she had found a higher calling than model, dancer, or actress. When Donna had broached the subject with him, he had pooh-poohed her intentions to put Molly in pageants, suggesting they were ridiculous and demeaning. Unfortunately, he hadn't lived long enough for them to even fight over it. Donna used to think she could have influenced his opinion, but she suspected otherwise. Molly was not quite three when he died, so it had never come between them. Very little had, in fact. Except for that darn police department.

They had planned on taking the kids to the Strawberry Festival in Plant City together, but he had been called into work at the last minute, so she had taken them without him. Although the annual festival was a ten-day event, his shift work and her school schedule had left them with one Saturday afternoon for them to all go together. But then the department had called and changed her plans for their weekend afternoon as a family. He never said "no" when the PD needed him.

The chief was sitting on their porch swing waiting for her when they had returned home. He had been there before, so the kids thought nothing of it. But she had known.

She had made it to the hospital in time to tell him she loved him, and then they had put him under anesthesia. He had flat-lined in surgery, and if it weren't for the children, she might have died with him.

She had kept every picture of him in the house in its place. She had slept with his shirts against her pillow until she could no longer detect his scent on his clothes. On her early-morning walks, she had held conversations with him in her head about the children, the plumbing, or any other random event until she realized she could no longer recall the sweet tenor of his voice. It had taken her three years to empty his closet and dresser drawers. She was certain she had looked at a picture of him at least once every day since the day he died, but she had finally started *living* without him — and his opinions.

She had done all she could to raise Molly to be a lady and to protect her from harm. And then, out of nowhere, Molly chose the most masculine, vulgar, and dangerous career Donna could imagine. She could only wonder why and how the best-laid plans had gone so terribly wrong.

Nick Monroe

He was running.

The asphalt was as black as the moonless night, and the air swam in his lungs. His shirt and shorts clung to his skin like a wet blanket, and his shoes were missing.

He had the night to himself, and he ran past houses and through grass pastures, across highways and parking lots, until he saw the clusters of metallic structures in the distance. His feet were bleeding and his muscles ached, but he did not mind, as long as he could save her this time. He ran toward the tin fortress piercing the skyline, pushing harder as a sliver of light caught the horizon, shading the path at his feet from black to gray to pink. His heartbeat echoed around him. If the sun came up before he reached her, it would be too late.

A chain-length fence erupted in front of him. It rattled as he climbed, his fingers and toes clinging to the metal, his body unbalanced by the unsteady links. The fence resisted his ascent, hissing against his weight, but he kept going. This time he knew where to find her. He wouldn't waste time in the main warehouse. He knew they had taken her to the juice-processing plant on the adjacent lot. If he hurried, he could get there before they began their assault.

Three rows of barbed wire lined the top of the fence. The vamps' voices bellowed around him—echoes of laughter, taunting him. And then he heard her scream. He reached for the highest row of wire and heaved himself over the fence, allowing its metal tips to slice his skin. The waist-high grass softened the ten-foot fall, but his heel landed on metal conduit. He swallowed the pain biting at his limbs as he frantically dug the cylinder from the weeds. He would need the weapon if he caught them. He begged the sun not to rise. Because then it would be too late. And she would make him promise. "Don't tell, Nicky. Please don't ever tell."

So he ran. He had to stop them. He had to protect her. But the earth was shaking. He could see the light of day rising over the old plant. And it was going to be too late. Again. He would always hear her screaming, "Nicky!"

He couldn't run anymore. He knew it was too late. She was lying on the cold concrete floor bruised and naked. He had only seen one of their faces, but it hadn't mattered because he was too late. They had gotten away with it. Because he had been too late. And she had begged him not to tell.

"Nicky!"

"I'm sorry, baby girl," he said.

"Honey, please wake up."

He heard his mother's voice, but the glare coming from the airplane window made it hard to open his eyes. "I'm awake, Ma."

"Thank goodness. You were having a bad dream. It must have been the turbulence."

"Yeah, you're probably right," he said.

He wished it had only been a dream.

About-Face

Poolee Molly Monroe

"First you bail on me when I'm in town, and now this. What's going on, Molly?"

"I didn't bail on you, John. I was sick."

"You can admit you had a hangover. I'm not your mom, you know."

"Hangovers don't last a week. I was worried I could be contagious. You should be glad I love you so much."

"And you should have given me a choice. And you should have known that I'm here for you – in good times and bad. I would have held your hair for you, no matter how awful you looked or how bad your vomit smelled."

"Ewww," Molly said. And she heard herself laughing – *a real laugh* – for the first time in a long time. This was one of many reasons she loved him. The thought *"in sickness and in health"* flashed through her mind, and she was glad they were having this discussion over the phone. He had a knack for seeing what she was thinking, and she didn't ever want him to know the truth about that week.

"Wait a second. Did you just say you love me?"

"You know I do. Don't act so surprised."

"But it's nice to hear you say it...wait. Is this a diversion tactic? Very clever, Miss Monroe."

"It's not a diversion. I do love you."

"If you love me so much, then why haven't I seen you all summer? And why can't you come up to Camp Lejeune for

a couple of weeks before you start school? I already put in for leave."

"I'm sorry about that, John. Can't you just postpone your leave, for say, about three months?"

"Are you kidding me? I've been looking forward to seeing you again. I miss you. If I didn't know better, I'd think you've been avoiding me."

"Don't think like that. I've missed you too. I've just been rethinking some things. But not about how I feel about you."

"Then what is it?"

"For starters, I'm not going to college. I've withdrawn from the program."

"What?"

"But I'll be nearby. Maybe you could visit me in South Carolina."

"Molly, cut to the chase already, and tell me what the hell is going on."

"I joined the Marine Corps, John. I ship tomorrow."

She had not been prepared for his response.

Corporal Trinity Baptiste

When Monroe walked into the female tent, everyone's eyes were on her. It was clear that she'd been outside the wire. All kinds of scuttlebutt was going around about what had happened, and Baptiste figured Monroe would want to talk about it eventually. As much as she wanted to know what went down, she didn't want to just plow into Monroe with questions. Monroe looked like she had bathed in blood and powder.

"Dang, girl, ya look worse for wear," Baptiste said.

"That's what I keep hearing," Monroe said. "Good thing I don't care how I look."

"Ya could look like the backside of a pig, and it wouldn't matter out here," Baptiste said.

"That's reassuring. Where's Jankowski?"

"What about the backside of a pig makes ya ask about her?"

"That's messed up, Baptiste."

"Yeah. Well, she went to chow as soon as they opened the hatches. She won't be back till she's full as a tick."

"Figures. We had planned to go for a run this evening. Who needs PT when you can stuff your face? Where's Ramirez?"

Baptiste was trying to think of a nice way to say that Monroe should know where Ramirez was when she answered her own stupid question.

"Oh, geez. Never mind. She's going to be there all freakin' night."

"That bad, huh?"

"Yeah. I guess I'll skip the run tonight." Monroe threw her towel, shower shoes, PT gear, and hygiene kit into a duffel bag. "They downed an Osprey. Twenty-two KIA is the number I got."

Dear Jesus, please be with their families, Baptiste thought. "*Ma chère*...I'm so sorry ya had to see that," she said. She pulled Monroe into a hug and held her tighter as Monroe swallowed a sob.

Monroe pulled away and said, "Thanks, Baptiste. But I need to write my story tonight. I'll see you later."

Baptiste watched her leave the tent with a heavy heart and then kneeled by her cot to pray.

First Lieutenant John Michaelson

John had an office to himself, but it was only a partition of a larger tent. He pulled the poncho liner hanging from the 550 cord that made up the walls of his office until it was taut, and he closed himself into his ten-foot-by-twelve-foot space. He wasn't alone in the tent, but it was the first time all day he had a sense of being alone, and he needed to think.

He had been bombarded with images of them together repeatedly in the Combat Operations Center. Their "firsts" had been looping in his head for hours.

He had first kissed her on July 4, 2007. He had gone with Nick, Beth, and Molly to the fireworks show at Tiger Stadium in Lakeland. She had stared at him with those crystal-blue eyes of hers with such intensity throughout the day that when the fireworks display began, he couldn't resist showing her how he felt. How ironic that their firsts had fallen on patriotic holidays. Ten months later, Nick, Beth, and Molly had come to see him at Camp Lejeune over Memorial Day weekend. After a day at the beach, she had snuck away with him to see his room in the officer's quarters. And they made love for the first time. For her first time.

He had already known that he wanted to marry her. That day had merely sealed the deal. She wasn't faking *old-fashioned*. She really was. He was certain he wouldn't find another girl so right for him. But he hadn't wanted to interfere with her plans for college. The way he saw it, they could keep the relationship going even better than they had with her living in Florida. North Carolina School of the Arts was easy driving distance from Camp Lejeune.

Then she seriously screwed everything up when she pulled an about-face.

He had known something odd was going on with her that summer. He had been down to see her graduate. He had played along with Nick and Molly, as he always did, pretending to just be "Nick's friend" in front of Donna. He had initially assumed it was because she would think he was too old for Molly, which was illogical since Nick was dating Beth, but Molly had finally explained Donna's issues with men in uniform to him.

He was planning on nixing that farce with Donna at some point that summer, but that never panned out. After the graduation ceremony, the four of them had plans for a week together at the beach. But Molly had gotten sick, and she would only let Nick and Beth in her room. He'd talked to her on the phone plenty during the week, but he'd had to return to the base without seeing her again. Then she had found excuses not to go see him at all throughout June and July. Just when he thought she was definitely heading north before starting college, she did a 180 on him. Sometimes he worried that maybe he had gotten her pregnant and that she'd had an abortion or something. He thought she was too conservative to do something like that, but what else would influence her impulsive behavior? She completely changed the direction of her life.

Two years ago, he had thought losing Molly was the worst thing he could endure. But having her here was absolutely killing him.

The craziest part of it all was that he was certain she still loved him. The simple fact remained unchanged. They weren't allowed to be together now. Overlooking the momentous detail that they were in a combat zone, where personal relations were prohibited, there was the nonnegotiable obstacle of rank structure. When she had enlisted in the Marine Corps, she had unintentionally made the decision to leave him. She couldn't have known then that officers and enlisted members are not permitted to have relationships, especially when it comes to dating. She wouldn't have known about Marine Corps regulations prohibiting fraternization.

He was convinced he would lose his commission if anyone found out about them, especially if he had been caught with her the year prior. She had contacted him, and he had tried not to meet her, but in the end, he couldn't resist seeing her. And he had been ashamed of himself for what had happened that night.

She had not been at Sergeant Hicks's debriefing, and it was all he could do to keep his thoughts focused on the assessment of the convoy's response to the crash. He had been interested in how Molly had conducted herself and couldn't help wondering how she was coping with it, but he couldn't let the others sense his interest in her. He had asked enough questions about each of the troops to allow himself a question or two about her, and he had been proud of her when Sergeant Hicks told him that she had saved the sole survivor's life. Sergeant Hicks had confided to him privately that Monroe had seemed a little rattled by the episode, but he had seen worse in some male Marines on their first exposure to death. Hicks said she had handled herself well considering the carnage at the scene. It took a lot to get any form of a complement from Sergeant Hicks, so John had been glad that she had carried her own weight out there. But he had badly wanted to see her.

How screwed up was it that twenty-two Marines had died that day, there was still a Marine missing, and all he could think about was Molly Monroe? He felt like such an ass.

He had done so well in the beginning of her tour here, keeping her away from his platoon and their missions, ensuring he wouldn't run into her on the camp. But now, tonight, he *needed* to see her. That was it. He wouldn't touch her or get too close, but he wouldn't be able to sleep tonight without seeing and speaking with her. He had no idea how to find out where she was without appearing unprofessional. He certainly couldn't go anywhere near the female tents. He couldn't imagine asking other Marines if they knew where she was; they would see right through him. What could an infantry officer possibly want with a female corporal from another battalion?

But maybe he could be extremely interested in the pictures. That was it. That would be his story. So the first place he would go looking for her was at work. Come to think of it, that was why Sergeant Hicks had told her she wasn't required at the briefing. She had said she would start on the story right away while it was still fresh.

He hoped she was at work. And he hoped he would find her alone. He didn't want to have to pretend not to care about her. Not tonight.

Lance Corporal Vanessa Ramirez

A lance corporal on the Quick Reaction Force had told her that there weren't any casualties from the convoy within her first five minutes at the crash site, and she had spent the rest of the afternoon and evening picking up body parts and personal effects. At first, she thought Molly should be glad that she had a friend who cared enough about her to subject herself to the live horror show. But as she spent the afternoon forming her case in her head, she started to feel like a jerk. First of all, Molly had spent hours at the crash site. And to top it off, Ramirez heard scuttlebutt that one of the guys on the bird had made it out alive, and "the female Marine on the convoy" had been the one to save him. Secondly, she watched the rest of her team and saw how they did this part as efficiently as the work they did at the hut, and it hit her like a slap in the face. This was her job. And she owed it to the fallen Marines to honor their sacrifices. She owed it to them to be here.

There was one Marine who had really gotten under her skin. His chevrons and name tag told her his name was Corporal Jones. His personal effects indicated he was a husband and father. And his facial expression told her that death had not come easily for him. He'd had a huge chunk of metal in his stomach, and he'd had a picture in his pocket of himself and—she could only assume—his wife and baby. The little boy couldn't have been more than a year old. She had felt connected to the corporal as she and Corporal Stanley tucked him into the body bag. She wished she could comfort him, have a conversation with him and maybe talk to him awhile about his son — learn the little boy's name.

She also realized the other Marines on the team were treating her a little differently. She didn't feel like such an outsider for a change. There was something nudging her gut that suggested maybe it was because she had finally volunteered to go outside the wire. Maybe they thought she had handled herself like a real Marine tonight. She realized this must be what Monroe had been after. They looked at you differently outside the wire. They showed respect. Maybe for once, she wasn't just a girl who happened to be a Marine. Maybe on this trip, she had actually become one of them. Only time would tell. But for tonight, it felt pretty good.

She couldn't wait to talk to Monroe about it

En Route

Poolee Molly Monroe

What was she thinking?

    Escape.

    The bus ride from Savannah to Parris Island was silent except for the low hum of the engine. The driver kept his eyes on the road and didn't acknowledge the presence of the forty-or-so disheveled teenagers on his bus. Most of the stale-smelling and wrinkled travelers were too tired or too scared to speak. The air was thick with the musky scents of the Savannah paper plant, the Beaufort County marshes, body odor, and the hint of rain that wanted to fall but had not been granted permission. Apparently air conditioning was a comfort they didn't deserve. Even though it was past midnight, the early-August breeze was hot and humid. The handful of open windows offered just enough draft to keep her skin from sticking to her clothes, but she could feel the sweat as it formed and pooled in the open spaces beneath her bra. She ignored the sweat inching its way toward her belly button; she sat motionless with her head pressed against the window.

    There were long stretches of darkness on the route from the airport to the island. She looked up hoping to see stars, but the sky was as black as the asphalt. For the first time in two months, the ice storm in her heart had thawed in bearable degrees, but now she could feel the ache in her chest — the pain that accompanies loss. She had finally done something that felt right, and it had upset everyone she loved.

    It was strange how one night could change everything.

She could see how her actions had seemed rash.

"You did what?" Her mother's shriek was intensified by the clatter of breaking glass against the kitchen tile floor.

Molly had moved quickly to pick up the pieces; her mother had stood still.

"Molly, stand up and look at me," she'd said.

Molly had obeyed but had trouble meeting her eyes. Instead, she had focused on the small red dot that had begun forming a squiggly line down her mother's left ankle. "Ma, you're cut."

"What happened to our plans, your plans, for college?"

Molly shrugged her shoulders.

"Didn't you think I might deserve consultation in a decision like this?"

Molly nodded her head "yes."

"So what were you thinking?"

Escape.

"Answer me!"

Molly closed her eyes against the tears. She couldn't answer.

"You do realize our country is at war, don't you?"

"But the recruiter said…"

"The recruiter will tell you whatever he has to so you'll sign your life away!" She had shouted and begun crying so hard she could no longer speak. She slumped into a kitchen chair, her anger apparently traded for despair.

Molly sat in the chair next to her, hands in her lap, legs crossed at the ankles, her head bowed as if she were praying. She waited for her mother to calm down.

"What's going on with you, Molly? You haven't seen any of your friends since graduation — and Beth? Have you spoken to Beth yet?"

Molly shook her head "no."

"You need to talk to her, Molly. She is your best friend, no matter what happened between Nick and her."

"I don't have time, Ma. I ship tomorrow."

Molly had kissed her mother on the cheek and run out of the kitchen. She could hear her telling her to "come back here right now" as she ran up the stairs. But she kept going and locked herself in her room. She simply had not known how to have that kind of conversation with her mother.

The bus stopped. A big red sign, bordered by palm trees, greeted the newcomers; it announced the entrance to Parris Island. The driver opened the doors, and a military policeman spoke in hushed tones with him as another one boarded the bus. He walked the aisle from the front to the back and then to the front again, studying each of them as if they were criminals. The Marine didn't speak. Then he got off the bus; the driver closed the doors, and they resumed speed.

There was one road onto the island, and as they crossed the bridge, Molly could tell that the tide was out. She could see that there was only silt where she had expected to see water. The smell of the mud was overbearing.

Her eyes had adjusted to the darkness, and she was long accustomed to the weight of humid air in her lungs. And it occurred to her then: she hadn't really been trying to escape a place. It was her own skin she needed to crawl out of.

Beth Bailey

The gunny had agreed to help her and was on the phone in his office. Sergeant Jackson had waited with her for a few minutes but had gone back out to the main office once she had proved she was calm.

"If you need anything, I'm right up front. Just let me know. Good to go?" Sergeant Jackson had patted her hand when he spoke.

"Sure. And thanks." Beth said. She couldn't help appreciating how good he looked in his uniform. She studied his physique as he walked away and decided he would look good out of uniform too. She could see how Molly had fallen for the hot-guy-in-a-uniform bit. Beth had been too infatuated with Nick to notice much of the military hoopla on their trips to North Carolina, but Molly had talked nonstop about how amazing John looked in uniform.

Beth had really missed Molly. They'd shared so much of their lives together; it didn't seem real that they had been estranged for so long. If it wasn't too late, she planned on patching things up with her. It didn't matter who was the most right or most wrong anymore.

"You said the music was incredible — and the light shows and the dancing. We're both dancers."

"I'm telling you, Molly. This isn't your crowd."

"How is it your crowd and not my crowd?"

"How about...it pushes the envelope of safe? It's not safe."

"But it's safe enough for you to do it?"

"It's just — I go on roller coasters, and drive faster than the speed limit, and party like there's no tomorrow, and my dad barely notices, much less cares. But you? Your mom and Nick would fight over who should kill me first."

"You're always telling me to live a little. And now that I want to, you're intentionally excluding me."

"This isn't a roller coaster, Molly. There are trolls who would see that you aren't rave ready — never will be — and could take advantage of that."

"Rave ready?"

"*You are not down for anything at any time. And if you were, you wouldn't be you. Why can't you just trust me on this?*"

"*Look, Beth, it's simple. I want to go. If you don't take me to one of these things with you, then I'm going to tell Nick about what you've been doing on the weekends he's out of town.*"

"*You would do that?*"

"*I shouldn't have to. We're blood sisters, remember?*"

"*There isn't another event until the night of graduation. The guys will be with us.*"

"*Then I guess we'll just have to tell them we need a girls' night out with our coffeehouse crew.*"

"*By 'we,' you mean me.*"

Molly didn't respond.

"*Fine,*" *Beth said.*

"*Good. It'll be fun. You'll see.*"

Beth thought of that old '90s song about the guy whose plane crashed the first time he flew. That's what that night was: a plane crash. And after that, it had turned into a colossal blame game. Beth realized now that Molly had been traumatized, but Beth had been so angry about being the scapegoat for what had happened and losing her relationship with Nick, she had not been the kind of friend Molly had needed. Tending to her physical wounds had not been enough.

Maybe she could be that kind of friend now.

If the gunny could tell Beth where Molly was, she would be there for her no matter what. She wondered whether it would be best to drive or fly. She guessed it depended on where Molly was. If Beth drove and got there too late, she wouldn't forgive herself. But if she flew and had to stay a while, getting around could get expensive.

The gunny came out of his office. He had been on the phone for almost an hour. When he finally emerged from his office, she was eager for anything he could tell her.

He sat with her on the bench in the hall. "All I can tell you is where she is. I don't know anything about her condition or how long she'll be there."

"I completely understand. Where is she?"

"Bethesda."

"Which is where exactly?"

"Maryland. It's one of the primary-care facilities for the military."

"And you're sure that's where she is? It would be awful to arrive and find out she's not there."

"Look. I can't make any promises, but a good friend of mine looked her up in the system. She's there *right now*. Here's the number to the hospital. Maybe they can tell you something."

She'd call and then catch the first flight out.

Syzygy

Lance Corporal Molly Monroe

The forecast had predicted heavy showers. The approaching syzygy had raised the tides, but the sun was descending into the dancing horizon with defiant radiance. As the ocean roared, the burnt-orange sun pushed white streaks of light upward and out of a magenta sky. Mammatus clouds could be seen in the distance, the aftermath of storms on distant shores. Molly closed her eyes and inhaled deeply. Nostalgia consumed her. So much had changed in a year. Would he come?

She could still feel the afterglow. Her skin stung in anticipation as the infrared rays of the sun were slowly replaced by the strength of a whipping wind. She opened her eyes and marveled at the eight-foot swells. She relished the cool splashes of sea spray against her hot skin. The foaming sea was violent and beautiful.

They were both Marines now. Anyone could tell by looking at him, but no one thought so much of her.

When she had called, he was quiet, polite. "Please come," she had said. She needed to know if he still loved her. And if he didn't, she needed to know that too.

The full moon was at her back. If she turned, she would see a white orb against royal blue. In a few hours more, the earth's shadow would fall upon the moon: a lunar eclipse during summer solstice.

It was ironic that perfect alignment could create such chaos.

Her heart sank with the setting sun. The red of the magenta hues faded into the sea, painting the sky purple and, finally, smoky gray. She turned toward the light of the moon and began walking the sandy path that led to her room.

And then she saw him. She couldn't see his hazel eyes, clipped brown hair, or chiseled features at this distance, but she recognized his lanky build and deliberate gait. He had walked with a sense of purpose for as long as she had known him. She slowed her step and willed herself to be calm. When he reached her, he stopped at arm's length in front of her.

"You came," she said.

"I didn't want to."

"You know I love you." She hadn't meant to say so.

"You shouldn't."

"Did you forget me so easily?" she asked. She took a step backward, determined not to cry.

"Have you forgotten everything you learned...Marine!" he said, gritting his teeth.

"You never even wrote to me!"

He shouted now. "You enlisted without telling me! You're the one who ended it!"

"I didn't know. You should have explained," she said. She felt her lips quiver, and she held back the emotion she felt pressing against her chest and throat.

He stepped closer, and his voice softened. He cradled her face with his hand and caressed her cheek with his thumb. "And then what, Molly? Please tell me how any explanation would have helped at that point. It was too late."

She knew he was right. But all she cared about right then was holding him close – if only for that moment.

First Lieutenant John Michaelson

He had waited in his two-door Ford pickup truck watching the outside of the Combat Camera tent. He could tell from the slit in the opening that there was a light, but he had no way of knowing whom he would encounter, so he had focused on keeping his composure. No matter who was in there, he'd have the same story. He was interested in the pictures taken. He wanted to learn more about what happened at the crash site. It was a perfectly legitimate request considering his Marines had been the first responders.

He was surprised when he entered the tent. She was alone. His tension morphed into adrenaline. He was finally alone with her.

She sat with her back to her desk, watching him. She was not facing her computer screen; she was reclined against the back of her chair, her legs stretched out in front of her, crossed at the ankles, as if she had been waiting for someone. She was wearing her utility trousers and green T-shirt, her cammie blouse slung over another chair. The computer was on, and there was a picture up on the screen. He could tell she had been crying. Her eyes looked smaller and had receded deeper into their sockets. Their blue had taken on a smoky gray and were glossy with the film of fresh tears. Beneath her puffy eyes, her cheeks and nose were bright red. But she looked like she was on the verge of a smile. "I heard the truck outside. I hoped it was you," she said.

He glanced at the picture. A close-up of half of Sergeant Hicks's face. He walked closer to the computer screen, and he could see the explosion through the windshield of the Humvee at a distance. He realized that the Intelligence team might be able to learn something from this picture, and he wondered what else she had captured with her lens. "I had hoped to see you at the debriefing," he said.

She stood up, and he had to take a step backward to keep from touching her. She inched closer and challenged him with her eyes; he could smell her fruit candy as she spoke. "I thought I'd be more useful here. Besides, I'm in no condition to pretend right now."

He pulled her close and hugged her, breathing her in. He hadn't expected this—hadn't prepared for it. He felt raw from the day. The ache from the fear of losing her had eaten its way through his chest. The surge of buried emotions plunged to the surface. He realized they were kissing. He was lost with her somewhere in North Carolina or Florida. Anywhere but this desert, in this uniform, performing his duties like a damned robot.

That thought brought him back to his surroundings. He held her face in his hands, his forehead against hers, her warm breath mingling with his own. "I was worried."

"I know," she said.

"I've missed you."

"I've missed you, too."

"I've tried so hard to understand why you did it. This is so impossible."

She grabbed a tight hold of his wrists and closed her eyes for so long that he was concerned he had said something to hurt her. But then she cleared her throat and said, "It's time I told you the truth about that week at the beach."

Lance Corporal Vanessa Ramirez

Vanessa stomped rather than walked the half-mile back to the tent with the two female sergeants she didn't know. She was so pissed she could punch someone in the face. Preferably Molly Monroe. It had been late when she had returned to camp, but instead of showering and hitting the rack when she realized Monroe wasn't at the hooch, she had put her flak jacket and helmet back on, and had left her tent without a battle buddy. The female Marines were not supposed to travel alone after the sun went down. Apparently there had been an epidemic of rapes in the camp lately, so rules had been established to protect them. Vanessa had wanted to talk to Monroe alone, so she didn't want anyone else tagging along. Besides, it had been too late to ask one of the other females to go with her, and she thought she would be returning with Monroe anyway, so as long as she didn't get caught on the way out, she would be okay. And she would have been. No one had seen her on the way to Monroe's office.

She had just passed the port-a-johns on her way back when the female sergeants had come out of nowhere and reamed her out. It had been all she could do not to tell them what she had seen in the Combat Camera tent. Here she was getting her ass chewed for something as stupid as not having a battle buddy with her, and Monroe was sucking face—and probably more than that by now—with some officer.

She wanted to puke. Wow! Little Miss Goody Two-Shoes, meritorious corporal; Molly Marine award winner in boot camp. She had pulled the wool over everyone's eyes, hadn't she? Vanessa wouldn't have believed it, except that she had seen it with her own two eyes.

She had been really quiet when she poked her head in the tent flap because if Sergeant Price had been there, he may have chewed her out about the battle-buddy bit himself. But with him, he would have just made her do some push-ups or something, and it would be no big deal. He'd probably even understand that after a day like today, the girls might need to talk alone, and might throw on his earbuds while he worked, or head over to the dining facility for some midnight rations — or pretend to, anyway. He was cool like that. So she had peered through the flap, real quiet-like, so she could prepare herself for her zero-dark-thirty excuse.

She hadn't been prepared to see some guy's tongue down Molly's throat. That was surprising enough. He was tall and lanky; no one she recognized, as far as she could tell from his profile. But when he turned just a bit and she saw the light gleam off the silver on his collar, she almost fell out. She backed away from the tent as quietly as she could and turned around and hauled ass. She couldn't get out of there fast enough.

Now her mind was racing. How long had this been going on? Had Molly been putting out to get missions? What was up with her and those Marines from Alpha Company? Who was that officer?

She hadn't been able to tell if he was a first lieutenant or a captain, but the silver bar or bars indicated one or the other. She would recognize him if she saw him again. She wondered if she should confront Monroe or just go straight to Sergeant Price. She and Monroe had been through a lot together; they'd been friends since boot camp. On one hand, she thought she should confront Monroe about it if, for no other reason, because of their friendship. But on the other, she didn't want to get talked into keeping her mouth shut. She was disgusted with Monroe's hypocrisy — that she acted so damned innocent and like she was such a good Marine, always trying to live up to that stupid statue, quoting leadership traits and principles. How about setting the freakin' example? Thinking about it made Ramirez's blood boil. She was leaning toward taking this to Sergeant Price. He'd know what to do.

But she'd sleep on it. She could deal with this shit in the morning.

Bitter Pill

Molly Monroe

She hadn't remembered much of what had happened before the darkness devoured her. Her memories were flashes of vivid colors, like splashes of ribbon dancing through the empty spaces from one thought to another. There were gaps between the light and feathering whispers of voices between the color bursts and the concrete.

What stayed with her was the pain.

She had awakened and recognized at once pain in her head and privates, but she didn't stir. She was afraid of where she might be.

She heard a click and then a closing door.

Then she heard Nick's voice near her. She had not felt his presence.

"How long before we have to wake her?"

"It's supposed to work in the first seventy-two hours, but they say the sooner the better," Beth said.

"Damn. It's already been about twelve hours since I found her."

"It's okay, babe. It'll work..."

"Don't you dare tell me it's okay. It's not okay! And don't call me that. I told you. We're getting her through this, and it's over. Do you hear me?"

"I heard you the first time. And I understand you're upset, but we need to talk..."

Molly opened her eyes. And Nick and Beth froze. She was in a hotel room. There was a dimly lit lamp on the far side of the room. The windows were closed, and there were cracks of sunlight at the seams of the window. Nick sat in a chair next to her bed. Beth had an open water bottle and a box in her hands. She sat on the bed and opened the box. Then she handed Molly a pill and the water.

"Everything hurts."

"You can have a painkiller in a minute, Molly bear. But you need to take this first. It'll keep you from having one of those bastards' baby."

Nick Monroe

"I'd like to freshen up before we go to baggage claim," Donna said.

He could tell by her tone that she was glad to be back on solid ground. "Yeah. Me too. I'll meet you outside the ladies' room in a few minutes."

He stared at his reflection with self-loathing. He splashed the cool water on his face and scrubbed it with his hands. Although his face wasn't flushed, he could feel the heat under his five o'clock shadow. He'd probably had one too many Jacks. Hell, he'd had more than a few too many over the last couple of years. To say he felt like a failure was putting it mildly. He had failed to protect Molly; he had failed to convince her to believe in the justice system; he had failed to find the leader of the crew—some loser named Buddy—and he had blamed Beth for all his failures.

He flinched when he remembered the last time he saw her.

"Nick, we have to talk about this!"

"There's nothing to talk about. You lied to me!"

"But I can explain! Please...it wasn't..."

"Don't you dare say it wasn't your fault! You've been dragging Molly into your dysfunctional way of life for as long as I've known you! I should have known from the beginning that you were trouble."

She turned away from him as if he'd slapped her. *"I never knew you could be so cruel."*

He had known his words would hurt her. Without saying so, he had implicitly indicted her for her mother's alcoholism and her father's stints in jail. Beth had been ashamed and embarrassed by her *"dysfunctional family"* for years and had felt more a part of the Monroe family than her own.

"You need to leave, Beth. And don't come back. You aren't welcome here anymore."

He hadn't forgiven himself for that failure either.

He looked at his phone. He *still* didn't have a signal.

Donna Monroe

She saw him from the top of the escalator as she and Nick made their way down to the baggage claim. The young man in a Marine uniform held a sign that said, "Monroe Family." She knew she had no right to resent him. He was here to help them, and he was just doing his job. But every time she saw the uniform, it reminded her that Molly had chosen the Marines over her. And it hurt.

As they drew closer to the austere young man, she raised her chin and attempted a smile. She subtly lifted her hand to get his attention, and they made eye contact.

Nick was on the stair just below her looking at his feet, so she leaned over his shoulder to point out the Marine to him. Then she noticed that he was staring intently at a message on his phone: *I'm going to Bethesda, Nick. Like it or not.*

Battle Buddy

Lance Corporal Molly Monroe

She was in a heavily wooded area, but she was still close enough to the ocean to smell it, even if she couldn't see it. She recognized the distinct mixture of fish, salt, and wet wood, and she remembered being here before, when the air was warm and her body was hot. Not in these dense woods, where she stood digging her fighting hole, staying in motion to keep the cold and damp evening breeze from clawing through her Gortex and sticking to her skin, but on the beach and in the arms of the man who held her heart.

She was in the field for night maneuvers during Marine Combat Training, which was the name for what they all simply called MCT. She was stationed at Camp Lejeune to complete her training, and every moment of every day, she was aware that John was sharing this 246-square-mile space with her. It was the closest she had been to him since her high-school graduation.

They were digging fighting holes outside of their defensive position. She expected a firefight simulation tonight.

"Uh, I think we're done, Monroe."

"Huh?" Molly stopped digging and looked up at the girl who had been her battle buddy in boot camp and again during MCT. Ramirez stood on top of the fighting hole with her hands on her hips. It was too dark to see more than her outline, but Molly could smell the cigarette stench on her uniform.

"*If you keep digging, you'll eventually hit water…I'll need to stand on an ammo can or some sand bags, as deep as you've gone,*" *Ramirez said with a laugh.*

"*Oh!*" *Molly laughed with her. She was standing in her hole and her eyes were level with the ground, but she was taller than Ramirez.*

"*You've been a machine all night, girl. You got an axe to grind or what? Somebody piss you off?*"

"*No.*" *Molly looked around for her war belt, pulled her canteen out of the pouch, and took a swig.*

"*Well, you're sure acting like it. We've probably got a few minutes before rounds come down range. And you know I'm a good listener.*"

"*It's nothing. It's a long story.*"

"*Spill it, Monroe. Or I'm gonna burn one cancer stick after another right here in the hole till you do.*"

Molly knew she would do it. Vanessa always found a way to use Molly's disgust of cigarette smoke against her. "*Okay. Well. Did I ever tell you I lost my virginity to a Marine?*"

"*What? When?*"

"*Last Memorial Day actually.*"

"*Get outta here. That's taking patriotism to the extreme.*"

"*Ha! I never thought about it like that. But that is pretty cool, now that you mention it.*"

"*So did you love him? Or was it just a one-night thing?*"

"*Oh. I loved him. Still love him.*"

"*Are you still together? Do I know him?*"

"*No and no.*"

"*So what happened?*"

"*Well. You know. Shit happens.*"

"*Bastard broke it off, didn't he?*"

"*No…yes…maybe…oh, hell. I don't know.*"

"You're making no sense, girl. Who broke up with who?"

"Whom. Who broke up with whom."

"Lay off the grammar, crackhead. You know what I mean."

"Yeah. I do. But I thought you'd want to know the correct way to…"

"Focus, girl. Focus. What I want is to hear the rest of this story. What happened between you two?"

Molly rolled her eyes at Vanessa's antics and shrugged her shoulders. "Well, everything was pretty amazing for a long time. We dated for a year or so, but…" Molly stared off in the distance.

"But what?"

"Something happened after I graduated, and I changed my mind about college."

"So…"

"I joined the Marine Corps."

"Obviously. What did he say?"

"He got really upset and didn't really explain why. He told me there was no future for us anymore."

"Well, that's messed up. I've heard of male Marines not wanting anything to do with female Marines, but that's some bullshit right there."

"It wasn't like that."

"Oh no? Then you're leaving something out, Beauty Queen."

"And you're a lot smarter than you look. Why do you try so hard to hide it?"

"Why are you changing the subject? Again."

"Because I was drugged and assaulted by a few guys, and it changed me. I never told him." Molly had not wanted to admit the truth to herself, much less anyone else. She looked around the woods to see if anyone else was nearby.

"Oh."

"What? Cat's got your tongue? That's a first. Didn't know you could be shocked!" Molly snapped. She felt an irrational rage.

"No. It's just — I'm sorry, Molly. That's some heavy shit. I don't even know what to say."

"Just drop it, okay." It had been a subject she had refused to discuss with even Nick. And now that the words were out there, she felt angry. She hadn't wanted pity from Ramirez or anyone. She had meant to tell Vanessa that John was an officer, but now she didn't feel like talking at all.

Molly was grateful when the sounds of blanks popping off around them exploded through the silence between them.

Corporal Trinity Baptiste

"Wake up, Monroe. Ya owe me a morning glory PT."

"Are you kidding me? You're gonna collect today?"

"Don't ya want to see the sunrise?" Baptiste felt a little devious. She'd heard Monroe come in a few hours ago, but since she'd had trouble sleeping herself, she figured Monroe was no better off than she was. Besides, she wanted to talk about what had gone down outside the wire yesterday. And she had waited long enough.

"Ah, ha-ha," Monroe whispered as she laced her shoes. "Since you're all motivated and ready to go, why don't you see if Ramirez and Jankowski want to join us? I'll brush my fangs and meet y'all at the hard top in ten."

"Sounds like a plan," Baptiste said, even though she knew she wasn't going to ask the others to join them. Monroe probably wouldn't open up about her experience in front of a group. She'd just pretend she hadn't been able to wake them. *A little white lie never hurt nobody*, she thought.

Sergeant Andrew Hicks

"I'm looking for volunteers," Sergeant Hicks said. When no one raised their hands, he realized they probably thought he had to assemble a working party. "So the Intel bubba's caught some great leads last night."

PFC Hart raised his hand.

"Well, PFC Hart is looking for some action, oorah!"

"Oorah! Yut, yut!" the squad barked.

"And they think they know where our MIA Marine is being held."

"Oorah! Yut, yut!" the squad barked louder.

"But how about I finish, war dogs?" Sergeant Hicks had to raise his voice to be heard above the hoopla. "The operations officer is looking for extra bodies as reinforcements to the lead element. Special Ops will have the lead on this one."

The rest of his squad raised their hands. "Good to go. Corporal Carter, you and PFC Hart are in. You can pick two more Marines to join us, and then all of you go on ahead and grab your trash. We have to be at the Combat Operations Center in fifteen minutes, so don't bother with chow yet. We'll hit the dining facility on the way out."

Lance Corporal Vanessa Ramirez

Vanessa tried to make sense of everything that had happened in the last twenty-four hours. It was so confusing. She had thought so much of Molly, had looked up to her. Just yesterday, she had been worried sick about her safety and had requested to do something that she had dreaded being forced to do for months. And Vanessa had finally felt like she had fit in with her platoon for doing it. She had felt grateful to Monroe for that. And she had hoped they would be able to share their experiences. Then there were the rumors that had spread like wildfire about Monroe saving a Marine's life. She had respected her like crazy for that one. But how was she supposed to get what she saw last night out of her head?

She needed someone to talk to. Maybe she could talk to Sergeant Price about it. Maybe she'd just speak "hypothetically" with him. She decided that was what she'd do. She'd stop by Combat Camera before heading over to the dining facility.

Limbo

Corporal Molly Monroe

The white mist enveloped her in a cocoon of warmth. She floated effortlessly without thought or emotion, without recognition of the confines of a body, unaware of her own essence, comprehending nothing but contentment within the translucent haze.

Sometimes the fog would clear, and like a curtain opening, she could see splashes of color and shapes of things, swirling patterns of beige and black, and chunks of pink and gray — substances she recognized but could not name — spiraling through a hot, white light. She could smell something cooking that she knew was not meant to be eaten. She could hear voices that coaxed her closer to the images. And she could feel her fleshy prison, biting and ripping her essence; and she recognized fear and pain and knew she could not stay, would not stay.

And she pulled away, willing the curtains to close, grateful for the numbing sensation and for the mist that shielded her from the sphere of images; they urged her to forget all that threatened her peaceful existence. And she complied.

Nick Monroe

He had not prepared himself properly for her condition. She was unrecognizable. Her head was swollen and wrapped in gauze; it even covered her left eye and cheekbone. She had tubes and wires connected to several parts of her body: a breathing tube, IV, catheter, and heart monitor. The room was cold and sterile, but the equipment was alive with its constant humming and beeping—more so, it seemed, than Molly.

Nick focused his attention on the CT and MRI films that Molly's doctor, Lieutenant Watson, had just explained to him, and he listened carefully as she continued. "One of our concerns is that Molly may have encountered two traumatic brain injuries within minutes of each other. There are two basic types of TBI—open-head injuries and closed-head injuries—and she may have experienced both in quick succession. We've been informed that she was not unconscious after the first blast, although she could have lost consciousness for a few seconds or even minutes and no one could have noticed, but we do know she participated in the first-response treatment to the wounded. Had that been the end of it, she may have walked away with a mild TBI. Mild TBI isn't as innocent as it sounds though. She could have experienced any number of symptoms such as fatigue, headaches, sleep or emotional disturbances, dizziness, seizures, nausea, or confusion, just to name a few. But because of recent guidelines, she would have been screened for TBI later that day, and she would have been treated as needed.

"The second blast occurred about thirty minutes after the first and originated from a Dumpster just outside the dining facility. She was in close proximity of the shrapnel and debris of the second detonation, and that's how she sustained the open-head injuries. Fortunately, there was already a large medical response at the scene, and since she was at Camp Leatherneck, where they have the best military medical facility in the country, she was stabilized and prepared for flight to Landstuhl Medical Center in Germany. There they performed a craniotomy to reduce the pressure to the brain caused by the hematoma here."

Nick had known a thing or two about TBI. He had played football since he was a kid, and plenty of players had experienced at least one concussion. But Molly looked worse off than any of his friends ever had, and he was afraid to ask the questions he knew needed to be asked. But he voiced them anyway.

"Do you think she'll live?"

"At this point, I think she stands a very good chance at survival."

"And what will her life be like? What are her chances at a full recovery?"

Lieutenant Watson was thoughtful for a moment. "It's hard to say until more of the swelling goes down. There are any number of facilities her injuries could interfere with, to include her emotions, impulse control, language, memory, and social behavior. They could affect her balance and recognition of body parts. There's a chance of hearing loss, language problems, and sensory problems. But honestly, we won't be able to determine the severity of her diagnosis until she wakes up."

Donna Monroe

"Lieutenant Watson has asked me to fill out a referral form for your family for the Fisher House, so if you could just fill in these blocks, I'll complete this section and fax it in...Mrs. Monroe?"

"I'm sorry, who? I didn't quite catch that," Donna said. She was having trouble taking it all in. She had been bombarded with paperwork since she arrived.

"Lieutenant Watson..."

"I'm sorry, ma'am. But I don't know who Lieutenant Watson is."

"Oh. I'm sorry. She's your daughter's doctor. You haven't met her yet?"

"Not yet." Donna had no interest in elaborating. She wasn't quite ready to deal with Molly's injuries. Nick would be there until she could; in the meantime, she had a mountain of red tape to cut through. "What exactly is the Fisher House, again?"

"It's a nearby home for families of wounded warriors to stay throughout the duration of their loved ones' recovery here. It's..."

"And how much will that cost?"

"It's free of charge, Mrs. Monroe. We just need to complete this referral form for you. Each family is allowed one suite, but we need to know how many of your family members will be here so they know what size unit to give you."

"Oh." It had been so much easier to be angry with the Marines. Despite their sympathetic words and efforts to help her, she couldn't let go of the fact that they had taken her baby from her. And their uniforms were a constant reminder of that. But it was harder with the hospital staff; they continued to surprise her with their kindness and helpfulness. She had desperately wanted to safeguard her anger. It was all she had to keep her from losing her sanity.

"Mrs. Monroe?"

Donna hadn't been in to see Molly yet. What if she died before she got there? What if the last memory Molly had of home was slamming the door in anger? What if Donna didn't have another chance to whisper in her baby's ear, like she had done every night after she had tucked her in, just to say, "Your mama loves you"? She had said it repeatedly when Molly was sleeping, hoping her girl would dream sweet dreams, knowing how much she was loved.

She needed to whisper in her baby's ear. She stood up, and she intended to tell the nurse that she was going to see her daughter right away. Instead, she heard a noise, like a whale in the ocean, and she felt a pain, like her chest was cracking open. Her vision blurred, and she felt the stranger in blue scrubs hugging her, and then she realized that she was the one making that wretched noise.

Gray Matter

Corporal Molly Monroe

"There's nothing to forgive, Molly. I just wish you would have trusted me. It wouldn't have changed how I felt about you."

"It didn't matter anymore how you felt about me. I hated myself."

"But it wasn't your fault."

"It felt like my fault. And it broke up Nick and Beth. And everything was ruined. I felt dirty. And nothing you or anyone could have said would have changed that."

"But knowing what I know now, I wish I had been there for you."

"That's kind of the problem, John. Nick has always been there for me. And Beth. And then you. And I was so ashamed. I needed to redeem myself in my own eyes. I respected you so much. I wanted to feel the same way about myself. I wanted to be the girl who didn't need everyone 'being there' for me. There are things in this world you and Nick can't protect me from, John. And the Marine Corps has been good for me in that way. I'm so much stronger than I was then. It's just — I realized today, when I was with that dying Marine...his name was Jones...Corporal Jones...he was in so much pain...and he knew...he knew he was..."

She thought she had cried herself dry, but her tears returned with renewed vigor.

"Shhhhh...I understand," he said, holding her closer.

She was grateful to have him there. She almost wished someone would see them together. She didn't want to pretend *not to love him anymore. "What are we going to do about us? How are we going to make this right?"*

"I haven't figured that out yet, Molly. But I'm not letting go of you ever again."

It was a strange sensation for her to willingly disobey an order. But at this moment, she could not convince her heart to feel guilt for being locked in the embrace of an officer.

Donna Monroe

"Your mama loves you," she whispered in Molly's ear. As soon as she had said it, she felt better, convinced Molly would hear her. But it was still disturbing to see her baby so swollen and wrapped in gauze. She pulled her chair closer to Molly's hospital bed and held her daughter's hand. "Well, she looks like she is in one piece," Donna said out loud.

"She might look like it, Ma. But we have to be prepared for a long recovery," Nick said, looking up from his book. He was lounging in a recliner near the door and had been reading when she had come into the room.

The nurse had shown her to the ladies' room, and Donna had cleaned her face and taken her prescription before the nurse showed her to Molly's hospital room. "What did the doctor say?"

"She explained a little bit about Molly's brain injuries. The primary damage was done to her frontal lobe, but she has secondary damage to her parietal and temporal lobes."

"So what does that mean?"

"She basically said it's difficult for her to predict the severity of damage, Ma. But she thinks we're going to be here awhile."

"Oh." Donna looked at all the equipment in the room and thought it seemed cold and impersonal. If Molly had to be here a while, then she would need to make it a more amenable place. She was about to tell Nick some of her ideas, but when she looked at him, his head was back in that book. "I don't know how you can sit over there and read at a time like this."

"I'm reading a book the doctor recommended, by some guy named Garry Prowe. I found it in the bookstore downstairs. *I'm* trying to learn about traumatic brain injury, Ma. One of us will need to if we are going to help her through this."

"No need to be so testy, Nicky. Or so mean. I'm going to help her through this too. I'm sorry I didn't realize what you were reading. What does it say?"

"Well, let me see...here's something for you. It says, 'Memory almost always is impaired by a brain injury. Four types of memory can be affected, singly or in combination:

1. Short-term: the ability to hold a small amount of information for about twenty seconds.

2. Long-term: the ability to hold and retrieve information for as little as a few days and as long as a few decades.

3. Retrograde: the ability to recall events that occurred prior to the injury.

4. Anterograde: the ability to recall events that occurred after the injury.'"

"Hmmm. That is interesting. Any idea what makes it temporary or permanent?"

"I haven't gotten too far yet, Ma. But it says every case is different."

"Well, our Molly's got a good attitude in everything she does. She'll snap out of this." She caught Nicky rolling his eyes, but she decided to ignore it.

"Here's something else, Ma: 'Two common, but usually temporary, cognitive complaints are confabulation and perseveration.'"

"I'm not a doctor, Nicky..."

"Let me finish...confabulation is the confusion of imagination and memory. The patient, struggling to explain the gaps in her memory and her bewilderment and fear as she emerges from her coma, creates a sometimes bizarre fantasy. Perseveration is the persistent repetition of a response—a word, a phrase, or a gesture, when the stimulus that triggered the response has disappeared. For example, the patient may respond to a question and then repeat the answer over and over, even well after the person who posed the question has left the room."

"Well, I suppose that is all good to know. I think I'll leave the reading to you though. I'm going to the gift shop. We've got to do something about this room."

She leaned down and kissed Molly's right cheek. "Your mama loves you," she whispered. She knew she would say so every chance she got. If she could give Molly sweet dreams by the sheer force of her will, she would.

Precipice

Recruit Molly Monroe

"...and grabbing the rope with your right hand, you're putting it in the small of your back."

"Aye, sir!"

"What hand is that?"

"Right hand, sir."

"You don't sound too confident. What hand is that?"

"Right hand, sir!"

"Now, like I showed you before, you are going to be locked into the D-ring. And you are going to freakin' repeat the ditty as such, one down!"

"One down!"

"One around."

"One around!"

"Two down."

"Two down!"

"Locking the gate."

"Locking the gate!"

"The gate is locked."

"The gate is locked!"

"From here, you're going to grab the rope in front with your left hand, which is known as?"

"Guide hand, sir!"

"Which is known as?"

"Guide hand, sir!"

"And from here you're going to lean back and touch that break with your?"

"Right hand, sir!"

"And you have that rope with your?"

"Guide hand, sir!"

"Now, when that black-shirt instructor tells you to, you're going to look over your right shoulder, and punching your right arm out to three o'clock, you're going to double-time it backward down my five-story wall, breaking once on the way down. Do you understand?"

"Yes, sir!"

"Simple! Is it not?"

"Yes, sir!"

"You don't sound too confident...my repel tower is simple! Is it not?"

"Yes, sir!"

Sergeant Brian Price

He had just finished reading the first draft of Corporal Monroe's article. He was impressed with her storytelling. She consistently wrote hard news stories as if they were human-interest pieces. She always managed to dive deeper into the *who* of the five *W*s of any newsworthy event than any of his other writers did. In this piece, she had described the Osprey crash to such an extent, he felt like he had been there himself. He had momentarily stopped reading while he waited for the lump in his throat and the rock in his chest to dissolve.

She had taken several pictures, although most of them would not be released to the public. She had apparently worked late into the night to finish the article. She had sent him an e-mail at 0200 with all her pictures attached but had informed him that the platoon commander had advised that several of the pictures would not be publishable, and the article would have to wait several days for publication—information he already knew. But he was still impressed with her dedication to duty. She was definitely a fire-and-forget Marine. He would give her a job to do, and she would do it (and then some) with little or no supervision.

As dependable as she was though, she drove him crazy. He was accustomed to having what he wanted without ever trying too hard. Usually, just being a nice guy with a southern accent and shit kickers was enough for him. It was all genuine, but he knew the effect he had on women. He rarely kept a girlfriend for very long, not because he and the girls didn't get along, but usually because he would become bored with them after a romp or two. He hadn't met anyone who really interested him, until Monroe.

At first, he thought it odd that she never flirted with him, until he realized how *ate up* she was with the Corps. She had first-class physical-fitness scores. She loved going to the rifle range. And she volunteered for the Marine Corps Martial Arts training every opportunity available. Heck, she was already a brown belt. And he thought that was hot—hot like Angelina-Jolie-in-*Tomb-Raider* hot. But Monroe didn't *look* tough like Jolie. Monroe looked sensitive and vulnerable, and he guessed that's why he had such a hard time seeing her as a Marine. She was all girl, and he knew firsthand how lovely she was underneath her uniform.

When she was promoted to corporal, she hosted a wet-down for their section. They had gone to a local club, and he had been the only guy who could dance—lucky for him—so had ended up spending the evening dancing with her. Eventually, he had talked her into going to a country bar with him alone. He had wanted to introduce her to mechanical-bull riding and honky-tonk music, and she was all about it. He had to persuade her to wait until after she watched him do it to get on the mechanical bull herself. He had never seen her laugh so much as when he picked himself off the mat. She had run up to him, kissed him on his cheek, given him a quick hug, and said, "Watch me. I've got this!"

She lasted four seconds on that bull and whooped and hollered the whole time. When he lifted her off the mat, he carried her straight to a barstool and kissed her fully on the mouth. He could still remember the taste of cranberry and Grey Goose on her lips.

When they closed the place down, they had shared a cab back to his barracks. And even after a night of dancing and bull riding, she still smelled like strawberries and shampoo. They had kissed for what had seemed like hours, and when he finally began unbuttoning her shirt, he had been sure she had wanted him to. But as he reached for her third button—the one that gave him a glimpse of her black, lace bra, barely concealing her creamy curves—her eyes had snapped open, and she had glared at him as if he had slapped her in the face. She had bolted so fast, he had not had time to ask what he had done wrong.

And when she had come to work on Monday, she had acted as if nothing in the world had happened between them.

"Good morning, Sergeant Price."

He jumped and felt his face go hot as he realized Ramirez had caught him daydreaming about her best friend. "Good morning, Lance Corporal Ramirez.

Corporal Monroe isn't in this morning. She'll probably be in later, if that's who you're looking for."

"Actually, I was looking for you, Sergeant. I was wondering if you could give me some advice."

"Sure thing. But you know, I was just about to head over to the dining facility. Have you eaten breakfast yet?"

"No, Sergeant."

"Then why don't we talk on the way? I have a vehicle. I'll give you a ride."

Reconciled

Corporal Molly Monroe

She was jogging. She did not notice the moon dust powdering her shoes. She turned up the volume and let her favorite combat-zone song guide her pace as she reveled in the beauty of the desert dawn.

She tried to sort through the roller coaster of emotions that the last twenty-four hours had provoked within her. The crash site had devastated her. And when she saw Brian, she knew he had wanted to comfort her, and she had wanted him to. She had longed to touch him, to hold him, and that confused and upset her, because she knew that she loved John. She worried over whether she could "just be friends" with Brian. She cared deeply for him and would be foolish to deny the magnetic attraction she felt when she was near him. She had treated him horribly for it, and she was ashamed. She worried about being around John. How would they reconcile his life as an officer and hers as enlisted? She had come to love her life as a Marine – almost as much as she loved him. She wondered what she would have to give up – her friendship, her career, her love? – because she knew she couldn't have it all.

The music pulsed through her veins. She could feel every nerve ending within herself. She focused on only one thought: John loved her, and her love for him nurtured her soul. As the sun burst though the endless sea of sand, her heartbeat leveled out, her pace strengthened, and she hoped his love was enough to chase away the phantoms that pursued her.

Beth Bailey

The nurse was putting something in Molly's IV.

"What are you giving her?" Nick asked.

"It's a painkiller...I'll have to clean the lacerations to her face again soon. How long do you need?" The nurse was gentle with her question.

Beth had not heard Nick's response. She stood frozen in the doorway to Molly's hospital room and had quietly stepped aside as the nurse left. Beth thought she had worked up the nerve for this moment in the days it had taken her to reach this point. Now that she was here, she was afraid. An onslaught of questions assaulted her. How badly was Molly injured? Would they ever be the friends they had once been? Would Nick even accept her being here? Would he make her leave? Could she handle this? Would she lose everything she had worked for at school? Her head screamed with questions she couldn't answer, but she stood silent, careful not to disturb the two people she still loved most in this world.

Molly's face was wrapped in gauze, and she had tubes running from all parts of her body to machines, which beeped with a steady rhythm. Nick was standing next to her bed, his head bowed, as he held her hand. His back was to the door.

Beth felt the tug at her heart, and she knew she needed to be there with them. A single tear crept down her cheek, and she braced herself for Nick's rejection. She eased to the opposite side of Molly's bed and intertwined her hand with Molly's, and she watched Nick's hold of Molly for his reaction. But there was none.

Seconds lapsed. And then minutes. And she felt his eyes on her.

She lifted her head to him, and the pain etched in his face broke her composure. He reached for her other hand, and they stood crying over Molly together.

Explosion

Corporal Molly Monroe

There had been no denying, since day one, that Sergeant Price had country-boy charm. He looked like James Dean and spoke with a southern drawl as smooth as Elvis. She hadn't felt so attracted to anyone since John. And John was still the only man she had willingly given herself to, in another lifetime, when she was only a girl in love.

As a Marine, she had found reasons to embrace everything that made her stronger, and ignoring her sensuality was one way to be strong. She focused on strengthening her body and her mind, PTing regularly, practicing Marine Corps Martial Arts, and learning all she could about being a Marine. She studied Marine Corps history and courtesies, memorized weapons nomenclature, and never let a male Marine open a door for her. She refused to be the weaker sex.

But Sergeant Price constantly reminded her that she was a girl. Not just with his even-tempered silky tone he used when he spoke to her but with his eyes. Sometimes, she resented it. She just wanted him to see her as another Marine – one of the guys, even. But other times it felt good to be desirable, to be wanted. She would have preferred to resist him and to stay focused on being strong. She told herself that wanting him was a weakness. But they worked together. And she genuinely liked him. He was easygoing and witty. She felt her barriers crumbling every time he made her laugh, which he did often. And she enjoyed his friendship, in spite of the sexual undercurrent.

And when she had become a noncommissioned officer (NCO), she had lost the Marine Corps reason to resist his advances. They were both NCOs, and although she wondered if that would mean they might not be allowed to work together anymore, she knew that a personal relationship between them wouldn't be considered unprofessional.

It had felt good to give in to him – to give in to herself, to be held. She had been willing to be a girl again, if only for one night. She had heard he was that type, and she hadn't held it against him. But just when she had decided to let go, to let him have her, to crave his touch, to let him satiate her longings, she heard a whisper in her ear, "You belong to me now, baby."

Her eyes had snapped open, "What?"

"Nothing. I didn't say anything. Now come back here, and let me kiss you, pretty little thing."

Her hands had begun to tremble, and she had hoped he didn't recognize the fear that overwhelmed her as she buttoned her shirt and backed away from him. It didn't matter what he had or hadn't said. Her phantoms had found her, and she wouldn't let them catch her again.

Sergeant Brian Price

The dining facility was large enough to feed Camp Leatherneck's masses, but it was separated into smaller sections fortified with sandbags and protective reinforcements—for the purpose of minimizing casualties in case of incoming mortars—so it would take obvious effort to find Monroe if she was in the dining facility. It was 0630 already. Many Marines were PTing, at work, or heading off camp by now, so the dining facility was not busy.

"Why don't we look around and see if Corporal Monroe is here?" he asked Ramirez.

"I don't know."

"I've got some questions about the story she wrote last night. She did a really good job on it, by the way. I can't wait to turn it in."

"That's good to go, Sergeant. I'm not surprised though; are you?"

He didn't have a chance to answer her before they rounded the corner and saw Monroe and the lieutenant from Alpha Company engrossed in conversation at a table off by themselves. Price glanced at Ramirez and pretended not to notice when her neck and face flushed. Price knew that Ramirez knew her hypothetical question was as obvious as the smile on Monroe's face. He was going to play extremely dumb on this one. It would be hard to keep his jealousy at bay, but he didn't want anyone to know his feelings for her, unless Molly changed her mind about him, of course.

He would deal with Monroe privately. Regardless of their previous intimacy, she had to know that he wouldn't tolerate fraternization in his section. Not even, or especially, from her.

First Lieutenant John Michaelson

He sat across from Molly at the dining facility with his back to the sandbag wall so he could see anyone coming in their direction. "We've got company," John said. "A sergeant and a lance corporal. I don't recognize either of them, but they are headed our way."

Molly stole a quick glance at them. "That would be Sergeant Price and Ramirez. I believe you've spoken with Sergeant Price quite a bit over the phone. When they walk up, you need to be going on and on about how great my story is, okay?"

"You're going to get a big head if I keep it up."

"But I like hearing it!"

"Noted, my little war pup," he whispered. He enjoyed watching her eyes light up in surprise at his term of endearment. He paused another beat before saying louder, "It was very well written, Corporal Monroe."

"Indeed it was, sir!" Sergeant Price said. The sergeant held on to the chair next to Molly as if he were saving the seat for himself. The lance corporal sat down in the seat next to John.

"Good morning, Marines," John said.

Sergeant Price held out his hand for a shake and said, "Good morning, sir. It's nice to finally meet you in person. I've seen you in some of the photos Lance Corporal Ryan took."

John returned the handshake and said, "Nice to meet you too, Sergeant. I've appreciated all the good press." John watched Sergeant Price as he sat in the seat next to Molly. He couldn't help noticing how possessive the sergeant seemed of her. He had pulled his chair a bit closer to her than the typical coworker would. John realized that Sergeant Price was a good-looking guy, and he had that "good ole boy" way about him that made some women swoon. John glanced at Molly to gauge her reaction to him and felt a streak of jealousy as he wondered if they had something going on between them. He'd ask Molly about Sergeant Price later.

If she saw the question in his expression, she ignored it. "This is Lance Corporal Ramirez," Molly said. She pointed to the chair at John's left.

"Oh." He turned to look at the lance corporal. "Hello. Nice to meet you too, Lance Corporal Ramirez."

"Uh. You too, uh, sir," she said with obviously faked enthusiasm.

He wondered what was going on. This whole exchange seemed like an act to him. He wondered if they were suspicious of him sitting with Molly; maybe the Marines could see their mutual attraction. He hoped he was just being paranoid. Some enlisted Marines were simply uncomfortable around officers.

The newcomers sat eating their food in awkward silence. He was the Marine not like the others, so he decided he'd head out. It was probably a good thing. He needed to get his head in the game. He had a big day ahead of him.

"Well, I have a mission to prep for. Thanks for the hard work, motivator." John hated leaving her already, but he would be leading his Marines in support of the Special Ops mission later. He hoped they wouldn't be too late for their missing Marine.

"My pleasure, sir. Be safe out there."

"You bet." He left the dining facility thankful that she would be inside the wire today.

Lance Corporal Vanessa Ramirez

She had no idea what to say. She wanted to talk to Monroe about everything, but Sergeant Price was here with them, and he was acting like Ramirez hadn't said a word this morning. There was no way he could be so dense as to not realize that she had been talking about Monroe on the drive to the dining facility. It was bad enough if he was going to ignore the wrongdoings of his meritorious Marine, but the way he was cozying up to her now, it looked like he was in some kind of competition with the lieutenant. What the hell was wrong with everyone? What a bunch of hypocrites.

"So you read my article already?" Molly asked Sergeant Price.

"Yeah. You really knocked this one out of the park. And you've got some great shots. That one with the Osprey going down is pretty incredible. Did you see that coming, or was it a coincidence?"

"You know, I thought the bird would be visible through the windshield, but it wasn't until I snapped the picture and felt the explosion that I realized what I had there."

Vanessa watched them in agitation. How had she misjudged him? Misjudged them both?

"Well, writing that story must have been good for you. You look a hell of a lot better than the last time I saw you. What's the secret? You got some magic potion?" Sergeant Price smiled and gave her a shoulder bump when he said it.

Molly blushed and got quiet.

He could really pour on the charm. Ramirez didn't know what it was about that Tennessee swagger that could be so appealing. She rolled her eyes and shook her head. Sergeant Price knew damned well what Monroe's magic potion was. She was doing the horizontal mambo in a freakin' combat zone with a commissioned officer, breaking every freakin' rule in the book. And he was sitting there all chummy like he thought he might be next. What a freakin' pig.

As Vanessa watched them looking at each other, she realized there was more between them than she had previously realized. It seemed like they were having an entire conversation between them without speaking out loud.

Monroe said, "By the way, I'm sorry I was such a jerk yesterday. The crash site messed me up for a while."

"It's okay. I figured as much," he said.

Molly looked toward the chow line, and smiled in recognition. "Oh look, there's Sergeant Hicks now," Molly said.

Vanessa turned to look as Molly waved to a red-headed, freckled sergeant with a muscular frame, loaded down with his battle rattle. He was with a group of Marines, all with their full combat loads, who looked like they were headed outside the wire. They were carrying to-go boxes. Sergeant Hicks nodded, threw her a friendly toss of his hand, and headed toward the exit hatch.

Vanessa looked back at Molly in time to see her mouth open in a silent scream, and Vanessa heard a commotion, and several Marines commanding everyone to "Get down!"

She looked back toward the shouting Marines and saw them tackle a dining-facility worker.

She turned back to Sergeant Price, who was looking in the direction of the commotion, in time to see him throw himself around Molly and push her under the table with him.

And then Vanessa felt herself go airborne as she was thrust from her seat by a wave of heat before slamming into the sandbag wall behind her.

Flash

Corporal Molly Monroe

Molly knew many things at once in the fractured moments before the explosion.

He was a local who worked in the dining facility. He had been friendly and handsome. She had spoken to him every time she went through the chow line, and she had been drawn to his deep-brown eyes and long lashes — the kind of lashes every woman wished she had naturally, before pressing them with a lash curler or applying mascara. She had often imagined him in America, wooing women with his shy demeanor and beautiful face.

In that instant, she had seen his face, and she knew he was terrified. She sensed he had been forced to do something terrible; his family was in danger. She felt his fear as if it were her own. And then it overwhelmed her when she looked at his chest and recognized the bulge beneath his white uniform.

And she saw Sergeant Hicks in his moment of recognition. He knew death was imminent. And he knew everyone in this partition of the DFAC was in grave danger. And he shouted, and his Marines shouted, and he threw himself at the terrified bomber, and his Marines followed him — as if it were a football game and they were tackling the player with the ball — piling atop him in a futile attempt to shield the diners from the blast.

And she felt protective arms around her, and she was maneuvered under the table, down to the deck, and she saw a flash of light, and she turned away from death and felt the blast of pressure wash over and around them. She felt her forehead hit the table leg, and she saw Vanessa land against the sand bag wall, and she squeezed her eyes shut against purple swirling sensations.

And when she opened her eyes, she knew she was alive, and Sergeant Price had protected her, and she felt gratitude, immediately followed by grief. Because Sergeant Hicks must be dead. And many Marines were hurt, including Vanessa. And then she swallowed back the pain in her skull and shoved all emotion out of reach, to a place where it would not interfere with her brain. She would need to think her way through this.

Donna Monroe

She had nearly dropped the flowers when she walked into Molly's room and had seen Beth and Nick holding hands with each other and Molly. She was so touched and overjoyed she had almost forgotten to put them on the windowsill before running over to hug Beth.

"Oh, sweetie. I'm so glad you came!" Donna had said, unable to control her cracking voice.

"Me too. I love y'all so much!" Beth had said, squeezing Donna in reply.

Since then, Beth and Donna had gone about making the room homier as Nick filled Beth in on Molly's condition. Beth had explained how she had brought her computer and some DVDs so that she could play music and movies that had been special to them growing up. Beth had several ideas about helping Molly wake up and for afterward, if Molly couldn't remember things.

"I tried to think of everything that would be helpful," Beth said as she took a photo album and framed pictures out of a small suitcase on wheels. She began placing five-by-seven frames on the windowsill.

Donna stopped fussing with her flowers and looked closer at the photos. She studied one in particular that confused her. She looked at Nick, and as soon as she caught his eyes, he looked away. She knew guilt when she saw it, and it was written all over his face. She had known her children had kept secrets from her, but she felt foolish for not realizing this one. She picked up the frame of the four friends, grouped into couples. John had obviously been more than just Nick's best friend. He had been Molly's boyfriend too, behind her back, of course.

"How long?" Donna said.

Beth gasped. "She still doesn't know?"

"It seemed irrelevant after the fact," Nick said to Beth, completely ignoring Donna's question.

"I said *how long*, Nicky."

"About a year, Ma. They started dating the summer before her senior year."

"And you kept it from me because…"

"Because you wouldn't have approved. And he was good to her."

Donna pointed at Molly, raising her voice unintentionally. "Do you call this being good to her? He's obviously the reason she joined!"

Beth started to cry again, and Nick shook his head.

Donna was furious. She could feel her chest and face burning. But Beth was becoming a teary mess already, and then Nicky bit his fist and started to pace. A single tear ran down his cheek. She was not accustomed to seeing her son get emotional. Fear gripped her, and instantly, there was no room for anger. She realized there was more to this, and it was downright worrisome. "What is it? What else haven't you told me?"

She had asked the questions, but she wasn't sure she really wanted to know.

When Beth guided her to a chair, she knew things were about to go south quickly.

911

Corporal Molly Monroe

They were standing on the tarmac waiting for the first plane of their twenty-seven-hour journey to Afghanistan. Their company commanders had each provided an accountability report, and the battalion commander called the formation to "Rest."

"First and foremost, Marines, I want you to know that I am going to do everything in my power to bring each and every one of you home on our return to the States. While I am committed to achieving one hundred percent mission accomplishment, I never lose sight of the fact that your welfare is in my hands. It is the thing that keeps me up at night; your safety throughout the duration of our deployment is my greatest hope. However, I am also a realist. And I know that our missions will be dangerous, and some of you may sacrifice your limbs or your life for our great nation.

"So take a good look around you, Marines. We may not all be here when our tour is up. I want you to make it your mission to take care of each other. Watch each other's backs. And be honorable in all that you do.

"No matter what you see, no matter what atrocities evoke anger in you, hold on to your core values: honor, courage, and commitment, to our God, our country, and our Corps.

"We are America's nine-one-one force. And it is our duty to protect not only the people of our country, but the ideals that made us the great nation we are today. Never forget

who you are, warriors! You are United States Marines! Oorah?"

"Oorah!" the formation replied in unison—as one thunderous rumble.

Sergeant Brian Price

The pain in his leg was unbearable. Something large and sharp was embedded in his right calf. He didn't want to turn over; whatever it was could get lodged in deeper.

"You okay, Monroe?"

"I can't breathe. You're heavy; think you could get off me now?"

He detected humor in her voice—a good indicator she was okay. He used his arms to take some of his weight off her and said, "I think you're going to have to crawl out from under me. I can't move my right leg. Something's in it."

She wiggled out from under him and crawled down toward his calf.

"Oh, geez."

"Well, don't leave me hanging. How bad is it?"

"It's a pretty big piece of metal, Sergeant."

"Well, if I'm about to lose my leg, the least you can do is remember that we're friends and cut the sergeant crap. Think you could do that?"

"You aren't going to lose your leg, Brian." And she crawled up toward him and looked him in the face. She softened her tone and said, "Thank you for protecting me from the blast, by the way."

He thought she might actually kiss him, but in a blink, she switched back into professional mode. "I just don't think I should remove that. You could lose a lot of blood real fast. I think the best thing is for me to find a corpsman and get you out of here. Can you hold still a minute while I check on Ramirez?"

"Sure." He watched Molly crawl out from under the table toward Ramirez. She looked like she was unconscious or dead. Her arm was twisted awkwardly behind her back. Molly checked her pulse and then began gently touching other parts of her body, apparently looking for broken bones or open wounds. Ramirez must still be alive. He watched Molly remove her own cammie blouse; then she placed Ramirez flat on her back and used it to secure Ramirez's arm against her body.

Then Molly turned to him and said, "I'll be right back, Brian. Please don't move."

First Lieutenant John Michaelson

He had turned around and headed back toward the direction he had just left and was running as fast as his legs would carry him. It had been less than five minutes since he had left the DFAC when he heard the explosion, and his first thought was Molly. And then he remembered that several of his Marines had been grabbing chow before stepping off. Then he heard the shrill base siren sounding and saw the medic vehicles and realized he wasn't the only one running toward the chaos.

He arrived quickly enough to not be deterred when he ran toward the damaged section of the building. As soon as he entered the hatch, he had to wait for his eyes to adjust, and he was assaulted with the smells of gunpowder, burned flesh, and the stench of open intestines. Through the hazy cloud, he could see that there were survivors, some walking dizzily and others checking people on the deck for wounds. He called out, but no one seemed to hear him.

He headed toward the corner table where he and Molly had been sitting, but he stumbled after his first step. He looked down and saw that he had tripped over a crater of flesh and debris. It took a second for his brain to register that the very spot he had passed minutes before—the same hatch he had exited, maybe ten minutes earlier—was the originating point of the explosion. In another half-second, he realized he was surrounded by camouflaged body parts, splashes of body fluid and tissue, flak jackets over solid chests, and the backside of a Marine bearing a name tape that said "Carter."

He studied the crater. He could see bits of flesh mingled with shredded plastic and white cotton material near the bottom of the hole. He knew instinctively that this explosion was the result of a suicide bomber, and these Marines had shielded the others from the brunt of the blast. He was hit by the act of bravery that had occurred here. These Marines had significantly reduced casualties. And they were his. He recognized their battle rattle. He was filled with pride and grief. He wanted to take a moment to mourn them, but there would be time for that later. "Thank you," he whispered, shoving his emotions out of his way. And then he stepped off to see who he could help.

Anamnesis

Corporal Molly Monroe

She was somewhere soft and light. She thought she might be swimming but not in water. A white mist enveloped her. So maybe she was floating – or flying. Yes. Maybe she was in the clouds.

Maybe she was dead. In heaven. With the angels.

And she heard music – so she listened. She wanted to sing; she had heard these notes before. And she had danced to them. She was a ballerina in the sky.

She tried to move closer to the music. The white became brighter, and then she felt cold. And her body ached. Her head hurt. Her eyes betrayed her, showing her images she did not want to see. She closed her eyes to the light and visions of limbs without bodies, and open eyes with no soul, and hearts with no beat. And the song in her voice became a scream, and she heard voices begging her to open her eyes, but she was afraid, and she would not listen.

And then she felt peace as the angels wrapped her in the warmth of their silky, silent, beautiful white mist.

Beth Bailey

Nick had taken Donna to their room at the Fisher House, and Beth stood alone—still shaken from the events of the morning—wondering how a family that had seemed so happy could keep so many secrets from one another. Maybe because they sheltered each other from ugly truths. Maybe they accepted the fragility of their happiness and chose not to acknowledge anything that could interfere with it. Perception is reality, and if you perceive no evil, there is none. Right?

Donna had not taken the news of Molly and John's relationship well, but it had paled in comparison to her reaction of the sexual assault on Molly. She had fallen to pieces. And Beth had felt guilty once again. Strangely enough to Beth though, Donna had blamed herself—not Beth. And then Nick had done the same. It seemed they all felt responsible for what had happened to Molly.

"And the assholes who really are to blame are still out there, Molly. Can you believe that?"

Why didn't we do something about it? Beth had asked herself the question often enough. But it was a rhetorical question because she knew the answer. Molly didn't want anyone to know that she had been raped. Molly had not even been able to say the word. She had refused to share the details with Beth and Nick, but they knew there had been multiple attackers. And Molly would have had to relive the event repeatedly and publicly to get justice.

She was thankful to have some time alone with Molly. "No matter what happens, we won't let anything come between us again." She curled her pinkie around Molly's and said, "Pinkie-swear?"

Beth wanted to believe Molly could hear her. If it weren't for the beeps and whooshes of the machines and all the gauze wrapped around her head, she could believe Molly was only sleeping. She had to hope her best friend was still inside her war-torn body. She was just resting and healing. Resting and healing.

"Resting and healing," Beth repeated it like a prayer. "She is just resting and healing."

Beth walked to the windowsill, where her iPod was docked and searched for her Michael Mikulin playlist. She turned the sound up enough to be heard above the machines in the room.

"Do you remember us, Molly? We were really good. Do you remember how Mrs. Walker let us come up with our own shows?"

Beth watched Molly for movement. She hoped for a sign, any signal that Molly could hear her.

"You would have loved the school of the arts. I've grown so much there. I can feel my creativity thriving, being surrounded by so much talent. And you," Beth shook away the threatening tears, "well, you. You would have blown them away."

As if to prove her point, a Mikulin song that Molly had used for one of their performances began playing. "Do you remember this, Molly? We got a standing ovation for this one, and we were only the opening act. I still remember every move of our dance."

Beth looked at Molly's face, the side that wasn't bandaged, and could have sworn she was smiling. But she doubted it. As much as she hoped for a sign, she knew she had to prepare herself for the worst: Molly might never wake up.

But then she heard a noise. It sounded almost like humming.

She stared at her friend. There was the slightest movement in her throat that suggested something beyond breathing, but it was hard to tell with that tube in her mouth. Beth returned to Molly's side and leaned in to listen. Yes! Molly was humming!

Beth hit the button to summon the nurse. This was great news!

"Molly, wake up, honey. Wake up. I'm here! It's me, Beth."

Beth couldn't contain her smile. Molly was waking. She would pull out of this!

Nurses rushed in and Beth said, "She hears me! She's humming to the music!" They scooted Beth out of the way, as they checked vitals and spoke to Molly, cajoling her to open her eyes.

Beth grabbed her cell phone and dialed Nick's number.

"Hello?"

And that's when Molly let loose a gargled scream.

After Blast

Corporal Molly Monroe

She didn't want to look at the crater. She knew what was in it or rather, who was in it. But first responders would be here soon, and they would need the battle-damage assessment. She would assist with the wounded first and give the corpsmen the information they would need to determine medical-evacuation priorities. After that, she would tell the investigators what she saw before the explosion.

"Molly! Thank God you're okay!"

"You too, uh, sir." Her automatic reaction was to look around to see if anyone else heard him. She was surprised he spoke so casually to her in public, even – no, especially – during a crisis. She knew she was thankful to see him, but she thought it was strange she didn't feel any emotional tug. He was smiling, and she thought maybe she should be too. But he hadn't just seen his Marines get blown to bits. Maybe her body knew she didn't have a right to feel the love she knew existed at a time like this. "I was about to do a battle-damage assessment for the first responders, but since you're here, sir, maybe we could move some of the wounded out."

She was glad when he switched back to being an officer instead of a boyfriend. "Let's go," he said.

First Lieutenant John Michaelson

He looked at his watch. It had only been twenty-eight minutes since the explosion, and there was already a flurry of activity around the dining facility. Medics, military police, and explosive-ordinance teams were on scene. Most of the Marines who had been eating in other sections of the DFAC had been cleared out already, and all the foreign-national workers had been detained. He and Molly, and some of the other Marines who had seen the bomber and were not seriously wounded, had been permitted to assist the first responders and asked to give accounts of what they had seen.

John had been impressed with Molly. It was still hard for him to see her as a Marine sometimes, but today, he had watched her tend to the wounded and listened to her describe gory details without emotion; he found little evidence of the girl who used to be accident-prone and queasy at the sight of blood. He watched her walk away from the Black Hawk that was taking off with Sergeant Price. His leg was in bad shape, and John wondered if they could save it. She acted unfazed by the whole scene, and he realized she was stronger than either of them had realized.

She was heading back to the dining facility, but he needed to get back to the Combat Operations Center. He was pretty certain his mission would still be a go, even if it had to be modified. He tried to ignore the image of his Marines in the crater that flashed in his mind. He would think about them later. He decided to intercept Molly so he could tell her good-bye.

And that's when the DFAC dipsy Dumpster burst into flames, propelling trash and metal shards toward everyone in the immediate vicinity. He shielded his face, just as he saw Molly crumble to the dirt.

Heroes

Corporal Molly Monroe

She ran through the beige moon dust, accustomed to the dry air and chalky sand that covered her shoes and powdered her legs. She welcomed the dawning of a new day, one day closer to humidity and greenery. She wanted to relax with a movie on a rainy afternoon and smell salt water on a sunny one, watching the crystal shimmers dancing across a sea-blue horizon.

"What are you doing here?" A voice interrupted her thoughts.

"What does it look like I'm doing? Same thing you are, Sergeant." Sergeant Hicks had surprised her, but she knew better than to let him see her with her guard down. Odd that she heard him over her iPod. He wasn't running in the Marine Corps green-on-green physical training clothes; he was in full-combat load. Strange, she thought. But it was a grunt thing to do. It seemed like the grunts always needed to prove they were tougher than the POGs and fobbits they shared the camp with. She hated the slang expressions grunts used. She couldn't help it that she was a "person other than a grunt," but she wasn't a Marine who never went outside the wire. She refused to be a fobbit!

"You don't belong here," he said.

Now that was pushing the limits. Some Marines might report him for that kind of remark. But she liked him, despite his male chauvinism, so she pretended she hadn't heard him, and she picked up her pace.

In spite of his uniform and equipment, he was easily keeping up with her. "Listen to me, Monroe!"

He was acting like a creeper, and she wanted to outrun him, but the faster she ran, the more persistent he became. "You have to leave. You don't belong here! Get out. Get out now, Monroe!"

And then she could feel the others chasing her.

Corporal Carter was closing in from behind. He screamed, "Watch out for the baby powder, Monroe. It's a trap!"

And she looked ahead and saw a white mist covering the sand, and the crashed Osprey, and boots kicking through the desert without legs, and she heard a man begging her to stop the pain. And she looked at his face, and she recognized him, but she knew no matter what she did, she would be unable to help him.

"I'm sorry!" she screamed, before running in the opposite direction. "I'm sorry; I can't help you." She felt pain burrowing in her chest, and she wanted to cry, but she knew crying would slow her speed. She couldn't think about them now. If she cried, she might hyperventilate, and she needed to run. The weight was heavy on her chest. She had to quit thinking about them. She needed to run faster. Refocus. Regroup. Breathe.

She turned away from the wreckage, and tried to outrun her pursuers.

But then she saw a crater, filled with blood and debris, and a once-beautiful face with dark-brown eyes and long, curled eyelashes, stretched into a leathery grimace. "Get out!" He was the one. The one with the big brown eyes, caramel complexion, and easy smile. The handsome DFAC worker. He had killed her friends.

Sergeant Hicks was dead. And so was Carter. They were all dead. "Get out!" Sergeant Hicks's bodiless head screamed at her. She looked in the crater filled with bone, flesh, and debris. Her friends were in pieces.

She kept thinking she needed to remember that. But she didn't want to.

"Listen to me!" he screamed like a girl.

She felt arms in the sand tugging on her feet.

"No!" She shouted as she kicked them away. She had to get out of this place.

"Wake up! Molly, it's me, Beth. Please wake up."

She opened her eyes and saw a blond girl crying at the edge of her bed.

"Oh, thank goodness, Molly! Are you okay?"

She could only see out of her right eye. And she felt restrained. Her head throbbed, her heart pounded against her chest, and her hands were shaking. But that didn't matter. Pain was weakness leaving the body, and fear merely an obstacle on the path to courage...she had heard that somewhere. The stranger was the problem. She thought to tell the blond girl to go away. She was confusing her with someone else. But the thought never made it to her lips. She closed her eyes and welcomed the silky blackness.

Private First Class Dakota Hart

Dakota's mom had kept trying to start up conversations with him, but he wasn't in the mood for chit-chat. He had only been stateside for a few days, and as glad as he might have been to see her, all he really wanted was to get back to his platoon. What was left of it, anyway. He was pretty sure that was never going to happen now. He glanced at his heavily bandaged left leg, and wondered if they were going to be able to keep any of the bloody pulp of a leg he last remembered seeing from the floor of the M-ATV.

He hated the medicine and disinfectant smells of the hospital, and he was up to his ears sick of everybody kissing his ass, especially while they continued telling him "*no*." It was hard as hell to not bite their heads off. He was still alive, and so many of his brothers were dead, and all the civilians around here acted like he was some kind of a hero. He wanted to get the hell out of this place.

But he had other things on his mind. He still had a promise to keep.

"Oh, hi, Nick. Come on in." His mother's voice startled him out of his thoughts. Some guy was at the door to his room, and his mom acted like she knew him. Dakota had never seen him before. He looked at her, silently requesting an explanation.

She said, "You asked me about Corporal Monroe yesterday. It turns out that her older brother, Nick is staying at the same place we are, Dakota. You know how I told you about the Fisher House? Several of the families from your platoon are there also."

Nick said, "Nice to meet you, Dakota."

Dakota said, "You too, Nick. How's Corporal Monroe?" Dakota studied him. Yeah. He could see it. This guy was a darker, taller, male version of Corporal Monroe. He figured the dark circles under the guy's eyes hadn't always been there. Dakota closed his eyes and tried to shut out the images of that day. Sergeant Hicks, Corporal Carter, and Corporal Murphy...Dakota would have been in that crater with them if he hadn't been conducting his vehicle checks. He had arrived shortly after the second explosion.

"She came out of the coma yesterday."

"That's good. Does she seem…normal?"

"Not quite. She hasn't spoken to us yet. And she has night terrors. She'll have a scar on her face. But the doctors say she's healing."

Dakota understood the night terrors. It was hard to get those images out of your head. But this guy already looked beat down. No sense in bringing that up. "She was a hard charger out there. She was with our unit when the Osprey crashed. Oh, wait. Has that been on the news?"

"Yes. That and the dining-facility attacks and the rescue of the missing Marine. Your unit has received a lot of media attention recently."

"He won't watch the news," his mom cut in, "and he won't let me turn it on, even if he's sleeping."

Dakota looked at his mom. If she didn't get out of his hospital room soon, he was going to end up hurting her feelings. "Mom, do you think I could have an iced tea and a piece of pie or something?" That would get her to the cafeteria for a while.

"Of course! I'll be back in a bit!" She grabbed her purse and seemed glad to have an excuse to get out. She probably wanted a cigarette.

Nick stared at the blank screen of the TV and said, "Yeah. I can relate to that. It's hard to watch sometimes." He looked away from Dakota. "My best friend was out there."

"Oh yeah? Was he at Leatherneck? It's a pretty big camp, but it's possible I knew him."

Nick eased into the recliner near the head of Dakota's bed and said, "I'm certain you do. But I'm not sure you want to talk about it."

"Try me."

"John Michaelson and I were best friends in college, and we continued to keep in touch after he joined the Marines."

Dakota heard the crack in Nick's voice. He felt his own chest constrict.

Nick rested his forehead in his hands, and even though he was looking at the deck, Dakota realized he was crying.

Everything made sense now, Dakota thought. He had seen Lt. Michaelson's reaction when Corporal Monroe was wounded. He thought back to the rescue mission and understood completely. Dakota needed to go see her, but he wasn't sure he could face her yet.

Dakota said, "I think if he wasn't my lieutenant, he'd be one of my closest friends too. He's the kind of officer that people respected *and* liked. Those traits don't always go together."

"Yeah, that doesn't surprise me," Nick said. "It was that way in college too. He was a bad-ass, but he sure knew how to have a good time."

Dakota smiled but felt his eyes burning. "I feel like I should have been able to do something. I feel like I let him down."

Nick said, "You can't blame yourself for what happened out there, Dakota. What matters is that you tried—you did everything you could—and you have to remember that. If you don't, you'll torture yourself with all the 'what ifs'. You'll dream of all the ways you could have saved those Marines. You'll lose sight of everything important in your life. You'll live in a fog of guilt. You could waste years drowning yourself in it."

Dakota wondered how this civilian understood what he was feeling. "Were you in the Corps too?"

"No."

Dakota waited for an explanation, but Nick looked over his shoulder toward the door and changed the subject. "Listen. Your mom has been talking to my mom, and she seems pretty worried about what you want to do."

"Yeah. She doesn't get it."

"I'm not sure any of us do, Dakota. Why on earth wouldn't you want to save your leg? Especially when the doctors are so optimistic about it?"

"The doctors aren't the ones who will have to live through the skin grafts, and the year or more of recovery. They aren't the ones stuck in this damn bed, in this God-forsaken hospital, while their best friends — their brothers — are getting shot. If I'm here, I'm not there! Don't you understand?"

"No. I don't understand how amputating your leg from the knee down gets you back to Afghanistan any sooner."

"Have you seen this pulp of a mess they're calling my leg?" Dakota said, pointing at his elevated left leg, wrapped in several inches of gauze. "It will take three times longer for it to heal than if they just cut the thing off and give me a prosthetic. I could be back on my feet and in the combat rotation within a year if I tried hard enough."

"Back on your *foot*. Think about what you're saying, Dakota."

"I have thought about it. I can get back to my unit faster without it! *That's all I'm saying!*"

Nick stood. "I have to get back to Molly, but..." He took a deep breath and let it go slowly, "I know if John were standing here right now, he would know what to say. He would know how to tell you that the year it takes to save your leg would be worth having it for the rest of your life. I respect you, Dakota. And I'm sure your platoon does too. You don't have to cut off your leg to prove your loyalty to them."

Nick stood to leave.

"Wait," Dakota said. "Could someone let me know when it would be a good time to go see Corporal Monroe?"

"Of course," Nick said.

"There is something I need to give her. It's in the drawer of the nightstand over there."

Nick opened the drawer and saw what was inside. He looked at Dakota and said, "So you knew about them?"

"No. I didn't really understand what that was about then. But I think I do now."

Nick nodded and said, "He had sent me one too. But it's a couple of months old. I take it yours is more recent?"

"Yeah. It was the last thing he said to me before we got the signal to go in."

Nick sighed. "I'm going to be away for the next few days. I'll let my mom know that you need to see Molly, and to make sure that you two have some privacy when you do."

"Thanks, Nick. Please send my regards."

"Yeah, man." Nick said. He left the room and closed the door.

Dakota looked at the remote control and clicked it on.

"CNN has verified the names of the dead and wounded Marines who participated in last week's daring rescue of Sergeant Rodney Walker, the Marine Corps machine gunner who had been taken prisoner in the Helmand province after falling from a crashing Osprey..."

He saw a picture of himself on the TV monitor, and he hit the mute button until it was gone.

Then he turned the volume back up.

"In other news, *Toy Story 3* is still running strong; last month, it became Pixar's highest-grossing film at the box office..."

He turned off the TV. "You hear that, sir!" he yelled to the empty room. "We rank right up there with the talking toys!" He threw the remote at the wall as hard as he could, and he felt better when it smashed into tiny little pieces.

Inamorata

Molly Monroe

Their bodies were still burning from the intensity of ocean and sun. Specks of white sand were coarse against tender, summer-tinted skin, and her hair was damp, falling in wavelets to the middle of her back. Her head pressed against the cold beige wall-locker; her back arched, as his lips lingered in the hollow of her throat; his forearms cradling her spine. She inhaled and savored the sweat and musk lingering under the sandy, coconut, salt-water, scent of him.

John lifted her easily and laid her on his neatly made bed. The brief absence of his body chilled her skin, and the austere surroundings of the officer quarters pierced the haze of her chaotic thoughts. Her lids fluttered open as he lowered his body toward hers, and she felt a flash of doubt when she stopped him with a gently placed foot.

"I'm not that kind of girl," she said.

"I know, Molly. That's why I love you."

She had known him long enough to believe him. They had been together for nearly a year, and he had never said those words before.

She thought her heart might explode. She wanted to belong to him fully, but she was unsure what to do. So she lowered her leg that held him back and pulled him into a kiss. "Show me," she whispered.

She welcomed the warmth of his body on hers and indulged the sensations surging beneath her skin. She hoped he knew that she loved him too.

Donna Monroe

"Your brother and Beth appear to be rekindling their relationship." Donna patted Molly's hand and stood up. "I always believed they belonged together."

She stared out the window. "By the way, Nick visited one of your friends the other day. They've been showing him on the news. They're calling him a hero."

She picked the picture up from the windowsill. "John is very handsome. I understand why you fell in love with him."

Donna walked toward Molly with the picture. "I just wish you would have told me. Was I really so unapproachable? Here I was thinking we were close, but it turns out you kept your life a secret from me."

Donna paced the room with the picture in her hands.

"I'm not upset about any of that anymore though. Not even your decision to join the Marine Corps. I understand that now. I just want you to get better. Do you hear me, hon? That's all that matters — that you get well."

She didn't feel quite so anxious now that she believed Molly was out of danger of dying. But she wondered how much of her daughter would be left once this was all over. Molly wasn't speaking yet, but she held on to the hope that most of her faculties would return eventually. Of course, when it came to her memory, it would be perfectly fine with Donna if Molly forgot all about that horrible night after graduation.

Donna wished she could forget it too, but at least it made sense of Molly's actions that summer. Maybe once Molly healed, she could go to college after all. Maybe she could even get back into North Carolina School of the Arts. If not, Donna could surely find a suitable program for her in Florida.

Healing would come first though. The doctors and nurses had been explaining the military's approach to emotional and physical therapy to her. Although they used too many acronyms for her liking, they were good about explaining themselves when she asked questions. They had also prepared her for an extended stay at the Fisher House.

She was okay with that. One of the nice things about staying at the Fisher House was meeting the other parents. Donna felt like she related to them right now even more than she did to Nick. They shared pictures and stories of their children and talked about their prognoses. They also shared their feelings. The other parents understood how hard it was to let go—to let one's child grow up and make their own decisions, no matter how risky or unwise they seemed. And how horrifying it was to know your own child was in mortal danger. They knew guilt, helplessness, and pain as intimately as she did.

"Excuse me, Mrs. Monroe?"

Donna had not realized someone else had entered the room. She turned to the door to see a nurse pushing a wheelchair carrying a young Latina with a neck brace and a cast on her arm. She looked to be about Molly's age.

"Yes?" Donna said.

The nurse said, "This is Vanessa. She's a friend of Molly's, and she wondered if she could visit for a few minutes."

Marine Times

Corporal Molly Monroe

"Are we clear?"

> *"Aye, Sergeant. No fruity lotion."*
>
> *"Or perfume or makeup…"*
>
> *"Understood."*
>
> *"Good," he said. "Then we're done here."*
>
> *"Would you mind explaining exactly what I've done to deserve your hostility, Sergeant?"*
>
> *"I don't have to explain anything to you, Corporal. But since you seem to be taking this personally, and I'm such a good guy, I'll break it down for you: you shouldn't be attached to infantry troops in a combat zone!"*
>
> *"You do know that statement could get you in a world of shit, don't you?"*
>
> *"A world of shit? Go for it, missy!"*
>
> *He was infuriating! She would have him by the balls before the sun went down, she decided.*
>
> *His face was as red as his hair. "You have no freakin' clue! Let me tell you about my world! In my world, convoys are funeral processions, and roving patrols are death marches. Until you see your best friend implode in front of you, I don't want to hear anything about a world of shit! I've been swimming in it since you were in middle school!"*
>
> *And then maybe she wouldn't. "I'm sorry to hear that, Sergeant. I really am. But I still don't understand why you dislike me so much."*

He looked away from her and muttered, "I don't dislike you, Monroe. You seem like a hard charger."

"Really? Then why do you treat me like I'm an outsider instead of a fellow NCO?"

He was quiet for several minutes. Finally, he sighed and said, "I'm not one of those politically correct Marines you're used to dealing with in Headquarters Company, so you're going to hear it straight from me. The truth is…no matter how hard you try, you will always be a little sister or potential girlfriend to my Marines. And out there," he pointed toward the area outside the camp, "you've either got big brothers trying to look out for their little sister or man whores trying to figure out how or when they can get down your pants, and they completely miss the AK-47s pointed at their faces."

"So you're saying if something goes wrong, it's my fault?"

"No. I'm saying that you — all of us — have to be on guard out there, and I can't have you or any of my Marines distracted with…"

"I can't help it if they have no discipline! Besides, I always carry my weight, Sergeant."

"Noted. But the real question is, can you carry anyone else's weight? What are you? About a buck twenty?"

"It doesn't matter how much I weigh! I learned how to fire my weapon and fight hand-to-hand just like any other Marine."

"I believe you can fire a weapon, Monroe. And maybe you can even fight. That isn't the issue."

"Then I don't get it."

"How are you going to carry a wounded male Marine to safety? Have you ever fireman-carried another Marine?"

"Yes."

"A male Marine?"

"No. But I did a fireman's-carry relay with Lance Corporal Ramirez once." She didn't mention how hard it was.

"So you were able to carry a girl your size on those scrawny little shoulders of yours? How do you think that would work with me on your shoulders?"

She didn't answer him.

"Here's another matter. What if you, Carter, and Murphy are all wounded in the same skirmish? Who do you think will be medevac'd first?"

"Whoever has the worst battle wounds."

"Annnnnhhh. Wrong. I've seen it with my own eyes, Monroe. Females without life-threatening wounds will still be on the first bird out."

"I don't believe you."

"You don't have to. But you asked."

She'd had enough. "Well, it sounds to me that I'm not the one with the problem, Sergeant! I guess you'd better make sure you and your Marines get your acts together, because I never asked for any special treatment!" she shouted.

"Noted. No special treatment out of my Marines or me. And no sweet little smiles coming outta you."

"Good," she said. "Then we're done here."

She stomped off so quickly, she completely missed his nod of approval.

Lance Corporal Vanessa Ramirez

They had heard Mrs. Monroe talking to Molly, but Vanessa figured the nurse hadn't wanted to embarrass her, so they had waited for a long pause to announce themselves.

"Oh, how lovely! Could you wheel her in over here?" Mrs. Monroe pointed to an open area near Molly's hospital bed and addressed Vanessa as the nurse pushed her through. "How long have you known Molly, dear?"

But Vanessa couldn't find her words. She was staring at the picture Mrs. Monroe had in her hands. She had held it against her body, but the picture was facing out, and at Vanessa's level in the wheelchair, she could see the faces perfectly. And she could feel puzzle pieces sliding into place...almost.

She had asked to come here to find out how Molly was doing and then tell Mrs. Monroe what an awesome Marine Molly was. Then she would give Molly and her family the pictures she brought, and the *Marine Times*. That was the plan, anyway. She and her nurse had discussed it this morning. They had practiced it actually.

Instead, she blurted out what was really on her mind. "Who's that?" She pointed to the picture in Mrs. Monroe's hands.

"Excuse me? Oh." Mrs. Monroe looked at the picture as if she had forgotten it was in her hands.

"Mrs. Monroe, could I show you something out here, real quick?" the nurse said, stopping short of the door. The nurse looked at Vanessa with concern and motioned for Mrs. Monroe to join her in the hallway.

Vanessa looked at Molly. Her head was wrapped on the side nearest her, so she couldn't see much of her face. Molly had looked normal when she was helping Vanessa after the explosion, from the bits and pieces she remembered. But she could have been dreaming. She thought someone had told her what happened to Molly, but she wasn't sure. She looked down at the newspaper she had in her lap. The front page had a close-up of that Alpha Company sergeant and a crashing Osprey in the background. It was a cool picture; probably a famous one by now. And Molly had taken it. She had written the story too. And it was in the *Marine Times*.

Vanessa heard the nurse say, "Are you sure it's okay if I leave her with you for a few moments?"

"Of course, it's fine," Mrs. Monroe said.

"Hit the call button if you need anything."

"We will be fine." Mrs. Monroe walked toward the window sill and placed the framed picture on it. "The nurse tells me you have a brain injury. Did you know Molly does too?"

"Yeah. But she looks way worse than me. Can I look at that picture please?"

Mrs. Monroe didn't seem to hear her. "From what I've learned, even a minor TBI can be serious. Were you unconscious for a while?"

"I'm fine. I'll go back to my unit soon."

"Are you happy about that, dear?"

"Well, no shit, Sherlock! How about the God-damned picture?"

Mrs. Monroe gasped and looked toward the door like she was waiting for someone to rescue her.

"Oh, geez. I'm sorry for swearing at you, ma'am."

Mrs. Monroe smiled and walked to the windowsill and began taking the picture out of the frame.

"Please, call me Donna." She pulled a chair close to Vanessa and sat down with her back toward Molly's bed. "How long have you known Molly, dear?"

"We were battle buddies in boot camp. Can I see that picture please?"

Donna turned the picture over so that she could remove the photograph and handed it to her without the frame. "Oh? What is a battle buddy?"

Vanessa said, "You watch each other's six."

"Oh. I see."

She doesn't get it, Vanessa thought.

"She joined the Marine Corps because she was raped," Vanessa said.

Mrs. Monroe had a strange look on her face. She shouldn't have said that. Why did she say that?

"So you were close then?"

Vanessa said, "I thought so. But I didn't know she was doing the horizontal mambo with the lieutenant. That's pretty jacked up, don't you think?"

Mrs. Monroe looked like she had thrown a grenade at her. Vanessa could tell she was jacking this convo up but good. She never knew what the hell was going to come out of her mouth anymore. "I'm sorry again. I don't mean to have such a potty mouth with you, ma'am."

Mrs. Monroe shook her head and chuckled. "No. I understand completely how you feel. She didn't tell me about him either, and she was dating him right under my nose. I knew he was Nick's friend, but I had no idea he and Molly were interested in each other." Mrs. Monroe kept staring at Vanessa's foot.

Vanessa was confused. She looked at her foot and realized she was tapping it again. Maybe that's what Mrs. Monroe was looking at. Then she remembered the picture she had in her hand. The picture startled her. She stared at it and wondered how Mrs. Monroe had a picture of the lieutenant and Molly together. They were with two other people she didn't recognize.

Mrs. Monroe said, "Nick is my son. Didn't Molly tell you about her older brother?"

"Yes. But how did he meet the lieutenant?"

"They went to college together," Mrs. Monroe said.

Something clicked with Vanessa. *Did I ever tell you I lost my virginity to a Marine?* "Well, I'll be damned! He's *that* guy!" Vanessa blurted.

She didn't notice the newspaper fall from her lap or Mrs. Monroe jump from her chair. The entire conversation she'd had with Molly in the fighting hole at Marine Combat Training came back to her in a rush. She wanted to kick herself in the ass; she had been such a jerk.

And then Vanessa remembered what the nurse said about the lieutenant a few minutes ago. "Now that's a freakin' tragedy, right there!"

Mrs. Monroe stooped down to pick the newspaper up from the deck. "What's this?" she said, holding the paper out in front of her.

The nurse poked her head in the room. "Everything okay in here?"

Vanessa was about to answer them both when a raspy whisper startled them all.

"Help," Molly said.

Beth Bailey

She and Nick had finished their dinner in the hospital cafeteria and were taking a salad back for Donna. She appreciated how easy it was to lace her hand with his. They hadn't verbally acknowledged it, but it was almost like they were dating again. What a strange place to rekindle their relationship.

She never would have guessed things would go this well with him when she left North Carolina. She came here expecting a fight. She came here for Molly. But he seemed glad to have her here, so she tried to inject optimism into the challenges they knew they would face with Molly. Beth had told Nick that this was a new beginning for the three of them and an opportunity to realign their priorities in their lives.

"I think sometimes we get so caught up with the whats, we forget about the whos."

"The whats? What are you talking about?" Nick asked.

"You know: what we do for a living, what we want to buy. Those *whats*. But it's the *whos* we have in our lives that really matter. Don't you think?"

Nick was about to answer her when they walked into Molly's room. He froze when he saw her.

Molly's bed was in a sitting position and her eye that wasn't bandaged was open. She was looking at Nick as they walked into the room.

Donna caught their attention and urged them closer to Molly's bed. "Come on in, Nick, Beth." When she made eye contact with them and subtly shook her head, Beth could tell something was wrong.

Donna glanced over at Molly and handed Beth a newspaper and some pictures. "A friend of Molly's came by a little while ago. She left these for us. They're from when they were in Afghanistan together."

Nick sat next to Molly on her bed and held her hand. "It's so good to see you awake. We were worried sick."

Molly stared at him.

Beth looked at the paper Donna had handed her, hoping to break the awkward silence. "This is a great shot, Molly. Your talent behind the camera is as good as it is in front of it."

Molly's open eye moved from Nick to Beth and back to Nick "Who are you?"

"I'm Nick, your brother."

This wasn't exactly the new beginning Beth had imagined.

Casualties

First Lieutenant John Michaelson

It was different this time. He had a feeling he couldn't shake.
"Hart."

"Yes, sir?"

"If I don't make it out of here, there's something I need you to do for me."

"You're gonna make it out of here, sir. We'll be back in the rear grilling dogs and drinking Yuengling before you know it."

"Yeah, maybe so. But just in case, let me know I can count on you."

"You have my word, sir."

"I have a letter in the left front pocket of my cammie blouse that needs to make it to Corporal Monroe," John said. "I need you to be discreet about it."

"Understood, sir," Hart said.

John appreciated that Hart didn't ask any questions, but he was considering explaining his request to him anyway. He was so sick of pretending she was just another Marine to him. But the radio squawked, "Avenging Eagle has landed. Do you copy?"

"Avenging Eagle has landed, copy. Birds of prey, en route, over," John responded on the radio.

"Let's go," he said to the rest of his team.

Corporal Trinity Baptiste

The camp was united in grief.

There was a formation of battlefield crosses: the rifles had been plunged into the sand, supported by sandbags. Each warrior's helmet rested on a rifle, with boots placed in front of the sandbags. Dog tags hung from the rifle grips.

At Camp Leatherneck, the battlefield-cross ceremony was usually a small, private affair, with just the Marines of that unit. But the last several days had resulted in many casualties in the camp. The back-to-back attacks had left little time for mourning.

The chaplain had requested a combined ceremony. "Soon," he had said. Too many had been affected. Too many were still in shock. The Marines needed closure in order to move on, he had urged. He had asked Corporal Baptiste to sing "Amazing Grace" at the end of the ceremony, and she had agreed to it.

It was an outdoor ceremony. Chairs had been placed in columns and rows for the units that had taken casualties. The warriors, mostly Marines, sat facing the battlefield crosses. Hundreds of Camp Leatherneck personnel—civilians, soldiers, sailors, and Marines—were standing in attendance behind them.

Trinity missed her friends. She needed them right now. But she knew this ceremony would have been horrible for Monroe and Ramirez, with Monroe so close to the deceased, and Ramirez processing these Marines' remains. Her friends must be at Bethesda by now. She hoped they would be okay.

Her thoughts became a stream of prayers. *Dear Jesus, please be with Monroe and Ramirez. Please let them live. Please help them recover. Wrap them in your love. Please be with these Marines. Comfort them. Please don't let me cry here, Lord. Please give me strength so they receive the gift of your grace.*

Each unit's first sergeant began calling roll. First they called the names of those in attendance, and each Marine responded "Present," loud and clear. Then the first sergeant called the names of the deceased.

"Sergeant Hicks!" the first sergeant called. *There was no response to his call.*

"Sergeant Andrew Hicks!" the first sergeant repeated. *There was no response.*

"Sergeant Andrew James Hicks!" the first sergeant repeated urgently. *Silence.*

Twelve of Alpha Company's Marines did not answer the call.

And Baptiste sang, "Amazing Grace, how sweet the sound..." Her voice cracked. *Help me sing this, Lord...for them.*

"...that saved a wretch like me..."

Corporal Molly Monroe

She could feel her body now. But she didn't feel herself. For once, she felt awake. Alert. Her throat was raw and gritty, and she could hear the steady rhythm of machines monitoring her vitals. Her head throbbed, but she had been given remote-control access to medication—she could feel it in her hand, the one without the IV—and when she pushed the button, it would ward off the pain. She heard a voice in the room, but she would not open her eyes. She would wait for the quiet first. They expected so much. They wanted her to speak to them. They wanted her to know them. But she didn't have strength for the effort of it.

Not that sleep was any easier. The faces that greeted her there were familiar, but they frightened her. They would mutilate themselves and each other and then taunt her with their blood and pain. They called to her from dark places. They wanted her to follow them, but Othello had warned her against them. He had reminded her that she was a warrior, and it was her duty to survive.

So she lay in her bed, awake, listening to a lady in the room. She liked listening to the people who stayed with her. They told good stories. The stories could keep her from dreaming for a little while.

Snapshots

Sergeant Brian Price

Monroe had not answered her phone or door all weekend, and she hadn't spoken to him outside of work for the entire week. But at work, she was as chipper as the Mouseketeers on a Disney cruise. There was no sign of the girl who had kissed him and then run in the early-Saturday-morning hours the weekend before. By Friday, he couldn't take it anymore.

"Hello, Sergeant Price."

"Hey, Monroe. I was just headed out for chow. Think I'm needing a meat and three today. Will you join me?"

"I'm not really hungry, Sergeant."

Brian edged closer to her and lowered his voice, "We need to talk. We are going to talk. And I think you'd rather do that at the restaurant than here, don't you?"

As soon as they got in his car he said, "So who was he?"

"What are you talking about?" *Molly asked.*

"Some guy must have broken your heart, but good," *Brian said.*

"Why do you say that?"

"Why do you answer my questions with a question, Molly? You know why I said it. Are we ever going to talk about Friday night? You can't just pretend it didn't happen."

"I think that would actually be best." *She tapped her fingers on the door and grabbed the handle like she was ready to bolt again.* "Just forget about all of it, Sergeant."

He put the car in gear, locked the doors, and began driving before she could change her mind. He said, "Well, I can't forget it. I don't want to. And we've been friends for too long for you to 'sergeant' me to death when we're alone. So please don't use Friday night as an excuse to distance yourself from me."

The minutes ticked by.

"C'mon, Molly, could you just level with me?"

She looked out the passenger window and didn't say anything, so he turned up the music and drove to their go-to place when he wanted a big lunch (with a meat and three sides). Just before he pulled into the parking lot, she turned down the music and said, "Look. I'm sorry, Brian. I had a bad experience, and I guess it messed me up pretty good."

"Do you want to talk about it?"

"No."

She looked like she was on the verge of tears, and Brian really didn't want that. As badly as he wanted to kiss her, he knew he needed to mend their friendship first. He decided then that he would wait, for as long as it took. He said, "Well, maybe we should talk about this instead," and he reached into the glove compartment and pulled out a picture he'd developed over the weekend.

When she saw herself on the mechanical bull, she had thrown her head back and laughed so hard that her shoulders shook. And that's when he knew their friendship was still good to go.

Corporal Molly Monroe

Molly's body felt light and airy, like she could float away, except for her head, which was throbbing and weighted down with something she couldn't identify. Her mouth felt like she had been eating chalk. She needed water. The room was quiet except for the beeping and humming of machines in her room. She tried to open her eyes and then remembered she could only open her right eye.

As the room came into focus, she realized there was a wheelchair parked by her bed, with a man sleeping in it. His chair was parallel to her bed, and he was facing her. His right leg, the one closest to her, was elevated and heavily bandaged. He was in a hospital gown. He was holding her hand.

She watched him as he slept. She couldn't see the color of his eyes, but they were deep set. He was handsome, she decided. He had brown hair, pouty lips, and chiseled features that reminded her of a famous movie star. But his name escaped her. He looked peaceful in his sleep. She didn't really want to disturb him, but she needed water badly.

She adjusted her hand slightly and began rubbing his wrist with her thumb. She tried to speak. "Hello," she said. Her voice cracked; it was only a whisper.

He shifted in the chair and sighed. He rolled his head in her direction and adjusted his grip on her hand. But his eyes were still closed.

"Thirsty," she said, louder this time.

His eyes opened. They were light brown, almost golden eyes—deep-set, beautiful brown eyes. "Molly, you're awake!" He smiled. She liked his smile. And his voice.

"Water, please?" she said.

"Yeah, sure thing." He shifted in his chair and rolled closer to a food cart in the corner. He poured a glass of water and then rolled himself and the cart closer to her bed. "I have to adjust your bed, okay?"

She tried to nod and then realized her head wouldn't move, so she spoke. "Thank you," she said.

He rolled himself as close to her as he could get with his leg extended. His foot was almost to the wall behind her. His waist was next to hers, and he smiled at her as he adjusted the bed and brought her upper body closer to him. Then he lifted the water to her mouth.

She took a long gulping drink of ice-cold water.

"Easy, Molly. You need to take it slowly," he said.

She really liked the sound of his voice. She knew she must know him. He seemed familiar to her. But she couldn't remember his name. "We're friends, aren't we?" He was so close to her. She liked studying his face. His smile was contagious.

"Yes. That we are."

"Tell me your name, and give me more water. Please."

His laughter was even better. "I'm Brian. Brian Price. And I brought you some pictures to help you remember what good friends we are." He inched closer to her when he offered her the water this time.

She greedily drank from the glass and knew she wanted to remember him.

Beth Bailey

Nick had been following Beth to Molly's room and stopped at the doorway when she did. There was a guy in a wheelchair who was parked on the right side of Molly's bed, and they were looking at pictures together. He was doing all the talking, pointing at the images and saying names, providing details of events. They looked very comfortable together. Molly appeared so responsive to him that it had momentarily stunned Beth. Molly appeared to be smiling, and Beth hated to interrupt that. She wondered if Molly had regained some of her memories.

Nick nudged Beth to go in the room, so she said, "Ahem, excuse me," as she entered. She set the stack of journals she had in her hand on the table next to the door and stopped midway in the room, still not wanting to intrude on the intimacy of Molly and her friend.

Molly was slow to turn her head — the bandage wrapped around the top and side covering her left eye was big and bulky — but Molly met Beth's statement with an alert right eye. It darted back and forth between Beth and Nick.

Nick set his stack of journals down on the table by the door and walked toward the guy in the wheelchair. He said, "Hi. I'm Nick. Molly's brother. I don't believe we've met."

"Brian Price. Pleased to meet you."

Nick grabbed Beth's hand and said, "And this is Beth. She and Molly were best friends in high school." Then he pulled her closer to him and said, "And she's my girlfriend."

Beth felt her face getting hot. It still felt new with Nick, and his statement surprised her.

"Nice to meet you, too, Beth," Brian said.

He had an easy way about him, and Beth decided she liked him.

Nick sat down on the bed on the other side of Brian and held on to Molly's left hand. "You look so much better today. How are you feeling?"

"Thirsty. And hungry. I think." Molly sounded hoarse, but it was music to Beth's ears. After a week of worrying, Beth was grateful she was finally showing signs of improvement. She wondered if Molly remembered any of their shared past together yet, but she was afraid to ask.

Nick must have read her mind. He asked, "Are you remembering anything yet?"

"I don't know yet. I see people in my dreams I think I knew. I think I remember most of what has happened since I woke up. Some of it is pretty foggy though."

"That's probably because of the drugs they have you on," Beth said.

"She knew we were friends," Brian said. He was all smiles when he said it. It was obvious to Beth that he cared for Molly — as more than a friend.

"I didn't know your name." Molly said it like she was teasing him.

"It's best you don't forget it again," he said with a wink.

Beth watched Nick as he turned his head away from them and pretended to cough. She could tell he was trying to hide his emotions. Molly must not remember John. Beth glanced around the room. The picture of the four of them wasn't on the windowsill anymore. She wondered why.

"Ahem. So, um, Molly. Beth and I are going to be away for a couple of days. Mom will still be here. As well as some of your friends, I think. But I um have some things I have to take care of. And then I'll be back. Okay?" Nick spoke like there was something stuck in his throat, but Beth felt like she was the only one in the room who understood what was going on. Brian and Molly seemed oblivious to his discomfort.

Molly said, "Okay."

Beth said, "A footlocker arrived for you today, Molly. Nick and I were the ones who cut the lock. We thought you might want to read some of your journals. We haven't opened or read any of them, just so you know." Beth glanced at Brian. "We thought they might have content too personal for you to want to share."

"Thank you," Molly said.

Nick said, "Thanks for going through your pictures with her, Brian. I hope it helps her get her memory back. But even if it doesn't..." He looked at Molly. "It's good to see you awake and smiling again, little sister." He kissed her on the forehead and said, "I'm going to send in a nurse so you can get some food. See you in a few days."

Nick stood up and reached for Beth's hand, and she walked out of the room with him. They went directly to the nurse's station and requested food for Molly's room. Then he guided Beth to the stairs, and when they reached a remote part of the stairwell, he pulled her into his arms and locked her in his embrace. His breath came in gulps. She realized he was trembling.

"I need a drink," he said.

"No, you don't, Nick. We'll get through this without it," she whispered.

She held him in silence until he regained his composure.

Journals

Recruit Vanessa Ramirez

Ramirez sat on the footlocker across from Monroe, reading her letters from home. Everybody in her family wrote to her, so she had a handful of mail every day. She tried to keep up with all of it, but she barely had enough time to write one letter to a different family member each day.

Their platoon was permitted about an hour of free time Monday through Saturday and four hours on Sunday. Most of the recruits used that time for letter writing or taking a decent shower. But Monroe used most of that time for writing in her diary.

"Why do you spend so much time in that journal of yours, Monroe? It's like Groundhog Day *here. How many times can you write, 'We PT'd, ate chow, studied Marine Corps knowledge, drilled, and cleaned our weapons today'?"*

Monroe closed her journal and used the key she kept on her dog-tag chain to lock it. "We qualified on the rifle range last week," Monroe said.

"All right, smart-ass. You know what I meant. Why don't you ever write home?"

"I do sometimes. But my mom's mad at me for being here, so my brother is the only one I really have to write to. I get a letter from him once a week, and I always write back."

"What's the deal with your mom?"

"I was supposed to go to college. I had been accepted to a really good performing-arts program, but I joined the Marine Corps instead. It didn't go over well when I told her."

"Performing arts, huh? Why does that not surprise me? Were you a dancer? What was your thang, girl?"

"I was a dancer, actor, and model. I took ballet and did some photo shoots, but I enjoyed acting on stage the most. My mom put me in a bunch of beauty pageants when I was a kid and kept it up all through high school. I didn't really like the pageants. The public-speaking part always scared the crap out of me."

"That's kind of weird. How could you like acting on stage but be afraid of public speaking?" Ramirez asked her.

"Well, when you're acting, all your words are scripted, and you aren't you. You're someone else. In a pageant, they are asking you questions about yourself, and you don't have a script."

"So how did you do in that part of the pageant?"

"Fine. I won several of the pageants I was in," Monroe said.

"Well, sounds like you didn't have anything to be afraid of after all, Beauty Queen."

Monroe shook her head and whispered, "Please don't call me that. I really don't want the other recruits to know about my past."

"All right." Ramirez shrugged her shoulders.

Monroe said, "The only reason I got through those pageants was because my mom researched every one of them and wrote a script for me, and then we practiced the Q&A together. In my head, I was always pretending to be someone else."

Ramirez felt sorry for Monroe. She decided she liked her and was going to ask some of her own family to write to her. The girl needed to get outside herself. Ramirez was about to change the subject, but before she got the chance, Staff Sergeant Martinez walked out of the drill instructor hut and did it for her. She hollered, "All right, you nasties, play time is *over! Get on your feet, now! Move! Five, four, three, two, one! You're done!"*

Corporal Molly Monroe

Molly had been reading her journals. There were several to get through, but she wanted to remember herself and her friends. Some of her friends had stopped by, but she wasn't sure who would be able to visit her — especially since several Marines in her unit were still deployed. The only Marines from Leatherneck who she knew were here were Ramirez and Sergeant Price, who were wounded the same day she was.

She was getting glimpses of herself. Some were triggered by what she read in her journals, and some of them would rise to the surface after a nap, which she seemed to need several times a day.

She had learned, in the short time since she had begun to remember, that there were gaps in time. Her memories were fragmented: scattered pieces of a puzzle. They were out of order, haphazard, chaotic. Some memories were fuzzy and others crystal-clear. She sometimes remembered her dreams, and sometimes she did not. But she was having trouble sorting through the truth and fiction in them. She believed she could trust her journals. They told her about herself and the people who mattered most in her life.

"What do you have there?" Sergeant Price wheeled himself into her room, looking like he was freshly showered and shaved.

"I've been reading my journals," Molly said.

"Oh, yeah? Got any juicy tidbits you want to share with me?"

Molly enjoyed his visits, but now that she had read about her relationships with John and Brian, she was confused. It was obvious that she had loved John and cared deeply for Brian, but she could only think about what she read. The feelings she had when she recorded her experiences in her journals seemed distant to her—like they had belonged to another person.

"So I read about that Saturday—the family-day event before we deployed," Molly said.

"And one of the kids was so big that he toppled over the bouncy house," Brian replied.

They both laughed, and Molly enjoyed the normality of it. "Tell me more," she said. She hoped that eventually she could feel her laughter on the inside.

Flesh and Blood

Corporal Trinity Baptiste

It was "lights out" in the tent, so they sat in the far corner, with their flashlights turned on but upside down so that the only light that filtered out of each one created a dim circle on the plywood floor. The four dim circles in the center of the group emitted just enough light for Baptiste to see the outlines of the three girls siting with their legs crossed, knee-to-knee with her in a tight circle.

"None of you have ever heard of the LaLaurie Mansion?" Baptiste whispered breathlessly.

Baptiste could tell that Ramirez, Jankowski, and Monroe were moving, probably shaking their heads, but only one of them whispered, "No. Tell us about it."

"It's only the most haunted house in New Orleans, with a most-brutal history behind it!" Baptiste continued. "Back in the early eighteen hundreds, Dr. LaLaurie and his wife owned the mansion. They were both distinguished and well-mannered and hosted some of the finest parties in the French Quarter. Their beautiful Creole home was maintained by dozens of slaves, but after some time, the neighbors started seeing that Mrs. LaLaurie mistreated her slaves. One neighbor saw the mistress chasing a little slave girl onto the roof of her house with a whip, and the girl was so scared, she jumped to her death. Later that day, the neighbor saw the mistress burying the child in her backyard."

Monroe gasped. "Please tell me this is just part of the ghost story, and it's not real."

Ramirez said, "Don't be so naïve, Monroe. They taught you about slavery in Florida, didn't they? Some pretty horrible shit happened."

"I'm not even done yet, okay?" Baptiste said. She lowered her voice and said, "The law was called, and when they saw what she had done, they impounded the slaves, and they were resold at auction. But the mistress had some relatives buy them back for her. Her neighbors reported later that slaves would enter her home and then never leave the house again. People knew about the LaLauries' mistreatment of slaves, but all that happened was people quit going to their parties."

Jankowski said, "It's horrible that people can turn a blind eye to unjust and inhumane treatment just because of ethnicity. You know, in Europe the Jews have suffered in similar ways. I don't understand what it is about humans that they can be so cruel to each other."

Baptiste said, "Well, it's the fallen angel who has free reign on Earth, ya know. He sings his serpent song, and poisons the mind of any who'll let 'im! That's why I look to our Father's Son, ma chère."

"Okay, can we skip the sermon, pastor, and get on with the story?" Ramirez said.

"One day," Baptiste continued, "there was a terrible fire in the kitchen. They think it was one of the slaves who was tryin' to kill 'imself. When the fire was out, the first responders discovered a secret door to the attic. What they found there scarred 'em for life."

"Let me guess—a bunch of dead slaves?" Ramirez asked.

"Worse," Baptiste said. "Tortured slaves. Some were alive, but most were dead. Dismembered body parts were scattered throughout the attic. There were men who had been castrated and women with their guts hangin' out. One woman's arms and legs had been cut off, but she was still alive."

Baptiste could hear Monroe sniffling. She reached across the circle and squeezed her hand.

"Did the slave owners go to jail?" Jankowski asked.

"No," Baptiste said. "They escaped that night and were never seen again. And anyone who has ever lived in tha' house since has heard 'em screaming and seen the tormented spirits. They say the ghosts cry for justice."

"The phantoms will always be there," Monroe said. "They will never see justice."

"But we can find justice for the living," Jankowski said.

"Not always," Monroe said.

"You need to lighten up, Beauty Queen," Ramirez said. "That happened over a hundred years ago. Shit's changing. Hell, we even have a black president now. At some point, we all have to let go of the past."

"But the past is part of our present, my friend," Baptiste said. "Not always so easy when you're the one who's been wronged."

Jankowski had started laughing when Baptiste spoke. "Wait, hold up. Beauty Queen? What's that all about?"

"Thanks, Ramirez!" Monroe slapped her friend's knee. "So much for keeping a secret." She started to stand and said, "That's a story for another day. I have to PT early tomorrow."

Jankowski grabbed her hand. "Wait."

Monroe sat down. "What?"

Jankowski took Baptiste's hand and said, "Girls, take Ramirez's hands."

When they were all holding hands, Jankowski said, "This is the part of the Corps I love. Our gunny told us once that we were all green. Some dark green and some light green but all green. And I believe it. Our skin color doesn't matter here."

"Skin matters less here, Ski, but it still matters. There are pockets of racism everywhere, even if your rose colored glasses keep you from seein' it. I know what you believe in your heart, and I love you for it," Baptiste said. "But that doesn't change reality."

"I see three girls who are very different from me, and I appreciate those differences, because knowing you makes me a better person," Monroe said. "I hope you don't think any of us hold prejudices, Baptiste. You're one of the kindest, coolest female Marines I know. And all Marines are cooler than civilians, so that puts you pretty high up there."

"Oh, brother," Ramirez grunted. "She's full of it tonight."

"Oh, hush, Ramirez. Quit ya pickin'! Y'all are like my own flesh and blood. Ya know that, right? No matter how much shade some folks throw at us, I won't forget what we have here. Do ya hear me now?"

"Shhh," someone grunted from across the room.

They all snickered.

Baptiste pulled them into a hug and whispered, "We're like gumbo, ya know? A unique dish, enriched by our diverse cultural influences, served together, to produce a most satisfying result."

"Mmm, gumbo sounds good right now," Jankowski whispered.

"You are just tryin' to rile me now, girl!" Baptiste said.

Ramirez said, "Thank God for Ski's bottomless pit; I can't handle anymore mush, Corporal!" She squeezed Baptiste's hand.

Baptiste said, "All right. We all need to hit the rack. We can't let Monroe PT by herself, ya know? We need to get some too!"

Jankowski groaned, which made the rest of them laugh.

Lance Corporal Vanessa Ramirez

The large chunk of metal that had protruded from his gut had been removed at the crash site. His face was frozen in its death mask: his eyes bulging and his mouth a grimace. Ramirez couldn't leave him like this while she worked. She closed his eyes and massaged his mouth into a relaxed position.

Then she began digging in his pockets for his personal effects. He had change in his right pocket. She picked up her clipboard and wrote, "Three quarters and one nickel." Then she dug in his left pocket and found a yellow sticky with some notes, a smooth gray rock, and a wedding ring. She recorded her findings and then dug through his cargo pockets. When she found the picture he had carried with him, she stared at a girl about her age holding a newborn in her arms. "I'm sorry," she whispered to the picture. Then she picked up her clipboard to note, "Three-by-five picture of woman and baby."

She surveyed his body and took note of his missing right foot. The flesh had been crushed, and the foot was not in solid shape, so it had not been collected with other body parts found at the site. She picked up her clipboard and used her black pen to color in the right foot on the human body drawing on the form.

"Go ahead and shade it black, Ramirez."

She jumped and screamed. He was sitting on the autopsy table, staring at her. There was blood oozing from his mouth, nose, and center of his chest. "Shade it all black, Ramirez," he said. "You're gone anyway. There's nothing left of you."

She looked at the forms on her clipboard. Her name and information was scribbled on the form, and the human-shaped drawing had been colored in with a black marker, over the head.

She dropped the clipboard and reached for her head. She couldn't feel it – it was gone!

"Vanessa, honey, wake up!"

Vanessa opened her eyes and stared into the blue-gray eyes of the red-headed nurse who spent so much time on her floor. She was adjusting Vanessa's bed.

Her heart was racing, and she didn't like it. She felt so angry!

The nurse was getting on her last nerve. Vanessa swore she woke her up every five minutes to poke at her or make her swallow some stupid pill she didn't need.

"That was a bad one, dear. Let me check your pulse and take your blood pressure, okay?"

Vanessa didn't know what she was talking about. She looked around the room. Still no visitors.

"Why won't you let anyone visit me here?" Vanessa asked.

"What do you mean, dear? Your mother just left a little while ago to get some food from the cafeteria," the nurse said.

Vanessa looked at the nurse. She didn't understand. She would remember her mother being with her. Wouldn't she?

The nurse said, "Remember, she told you that some of your aunts would be coming down to see you later in the week? She told me all about your family and how proud they all are of you."

Vanessa looked closer at her room. There was a sweater she didn't recognize hanging over a chair and an empty paper cup that looked like it would disintegrate from the moisture at the bottom, as well as a folded magazine placed on the table in the corner by the recliner.

She glanced at the nurse, who was studying her.

"Oh yeah, that's right," Vanessa said. She tried to laugh it off, but her voice sounded all wrong.

She felt her bed shaking and looked down at her foot. It was spazzing out on her. She needed to get out of this place. She wanted to get back to her unit. This place was messing with her head.

"I miss my friends," she said.

Reflection

Corporal Molly Monroe

She stood on the dock of a red river. The beautiful man was dressed in all white.

"Why did you do it?" Molly asked him.

"You already know the answer."

"They threatened your family?"

"Of course…that is what you would like me to say?"

Molly said, "Are the other workers' families in danger?"

"Only the locals, but your government brings in foreigners now. This you already know."

"You killed my friends."

"They too were killers."

"You could have killed me, but I did nothing to you."

"And you would kill me to save those you love, wouldn't you?"

Molly hesitated, but she knew her answer. "Yes."

"Then we are not much different, are we?" And he scratched at his face and tore at his skin, ripping away the beautiful flesh. And he peeled it back, so nothing human remained, and his teeth grew fangs, and his hands had claws, and the animal growled and lunged at her. She felt the pain from his claws as they slashed her face, and she heard herself screaming. He was killing her! He growled, "You are the monster now!" And with each slash, he said, "You are a killer…a killer…infidel!"

And in a faraway place, a woman asked, "What is that?" Another voice answered, "It's a painkiller."
And the monster melted away.

Donna Monroe

Donna had been alone with Molly all morning. She had watched her in her sleep, knew she was having nightmares, and wished she could do more to help her. Donna appreciated having some time to herself for a change. Molly's hospital room had started to remind her of a coffee shop. Every time she came in here, Molly had visitors, whether she was awake or asleep.

Donna was beginning to wonder if she had ever really known her daughter at all. Her life was so different from what she had imagined. Molly's friends would tell her stories about boot camp or Camp Leatherneck and would show her articles Molly had written or pictures she had taken. Donna continued to find herself surprised and impressed with her daughter's courage and talents. She had always pushed Molly to be in front of the camera but never imagined her behind it. She was beginning to realize that there was truly no going back to Molly's former life. She had fooled herself to think that Molly could just go back to being the girl she was in high school, after everything she had experienced.

Donna had spent enough time now with the wounded Marines and their families to realize how very different Molly's lifestyle had been and how severely she was wounded. Donna's hopes and prayers now rested on Molly being able to regain her memory and ability to walk. Donna decided that whatever Molly wanted to do after that would be her decision. She vowed to herself to make no suggestions about what Molly should do with the rest of her life, unless Molly requested them.

The doctors here had been keeping Donna informed about Molly's progress. There was plenty to be optimistic about. The swelling in her brain was going down, and they could tell by her responses when she was awake that she was forming new memories. And while her retrograde amnesia was pretty severe, in that she had woken from the coma with no memories of her past, there was a strong possibility that she might remember most of her forgotten memories. The doctors suggested that the events closest to the trauma were the ones most likely to be forgotten completely, and that was just fine with Donna. Unfortunately, Molly was suffering from night terrors in her sleep, so she would require therapy to deal with the emotional trauma she had experienced.

Donna thought about both of her children and realized how much stronger they were than she had ever realized. She had been unaware of how much responsibility she had placed on Nick, until she began learning about all the ways he tried to protect Molly. And she admired the strength and willpower that she had not previously noticed in her daughter.

Corporal Molly Monroe

Something woke her, but she wasn't sure what it was. The monitors continued their beeping, and her head still felt like it weighed a ton. When she opened her right eye, she saw that her mother was sleeping in the recliner.

She felt a single sensation of happiness. She had a fleeting memory of seeing her mother sleeping on her couch at home in Florida.

"Hello, Molly." A lady spoke and startled her. The voice was behind her, on the side that couldn't see. She moved to the right side of the bed, and Molly remembered seeing this nurse before, although she didn't know or remember her name. She remembered her for her sugary West Virginia accent. "How are you feeling?" the nurse said.

"The light's too bright, my head has an elephant sitting on it, and I think I've been drinking sand. Other than that, I'm doing great, thanks."

The nurse laughed, and her mother woke up. The nurse walked to the window and closed the curtains. "Better?"

"Yes, thank you."

"I need to redress your bandage, sweetie. You okay with that?"

"Yes, but could I please have some water first?"

Her mom said, "I'll get it, Susan."

Molly took note of the nurse's name, and said, "Susan, do you think I could get a painkiller that doesn't make me dopey? I don't like sleeping so much anymore."

"Of course, dear. Donna, could you adjust Molly's bed while I get her some meds? I'll be right back."

Her mom adjusted her bed and helped her drink the full glass of water.

"I remember walking around with a book on my head, Ma," she said. "In fact, I don't know when my memory started creeping back in, but I remember a lot of things about home."

"Oh, hon, that's wonderful news!" her mom said. She squeezed Molly's hand when she spoke.

Molly wondered if anyone had told John what had happened to her. She wondered if he would be, or had been, here to visit her. She didn't want to mention it to her mom though, because she had never told her about John. Maybe she would later but not yet. Her mom seemed okay for now, but Molly had seen her flip out about things before, and she wasn't ready to deal with that yet.

Nick had told her he needed to go somewhere for a while, but she couldn't remember how long ago that had been. He would know what was going on with John. She would ask Beth or Nick when they returned.

"When's Nicky coming back, Ma?"

"Oh…he'll be back tomorrow, hon."

"Is something wrong?" Molly asked. She didn't understand why her mom looked like she was about to cry.

Donna fidgeted in her chair and then shook her head. "He had to go take care of something important to him. I'm sure he'll talk to you about it if you ask him."

Susan returned and handed Molly an eight-hundred-milligram Motrin, which made her smile.

"Marine candy" was one of their names for it. "Good ole vitamin M," she said. It made her feel like she was on the path to recovery.

Susan began unwrapping the gauze from around Molly's head. Molly kept her eye on her mother's face. She looked a little scared. When her head was completely unwrapped, Molly opened her left eye. She was relieved to realize she could see out of it.

"This will be a little cold," the nurse said. "I'm just cleaning the wound." She relaxed her eyelids and resisted the urge to sleep again. She didn't want to sleep. The cold air and wet cloth against her face left strange sensations.

"When will the swelling be gone?" Donna asked.

"It's already gone down quite a bit," Susan said. "But that could take another week or so."

Molly realized that she hadn't seen herself since…since she couldn't remember when.

"I want to see," Molly said.

Donna looked at the nurse. "You might want to wait…"

"No. It's okay, Ma," Molly interrupted. "I'm ready for this."

When the nurse handed her the mirror, she realized she was wrong. She wasn't prepared for her reflection.

Lance Corporal Vanessa Ramirez

The red-headed nursed wheeled her into Monroe's hospital room in time for Vanessa to catch her checking out the swollen, shaved side of her head and the jagged scar that ran like a lightning bolt down Monroe's cheek. Molly's face said it all. You would have thought she was Frankenstein. "Well, hello there, Beauty Queen!" Ramirez said.

Molly put down the mirror and a hundred emotions flashed on her face before she settled on a smile. "Hello...Ramirez?"

"Yeah. Ha! I knew you wouldn't forget me, girl!" Vanessa said as the nurse rolled her wheelchair closer to Monroe's bed.

Monroe shrugged her shoulders and scrunched her nose. "Well, you're the only one who calls me that ridiculous name."

"Yeah, well, I'm not the one who made you participate in those ridiculous pageants," Ramirez quipped.

"Um, that would be me."

Ramirez wheeled around to see a lady in the recliner by the window.

"Oh, I'm sorry. I didn't know anyone else was here."

"It's okay, Vanessa," the lady said. "It's good to see you again."

Vanessa was confused. She didn't remember seeing her before...but she must be Molly's mom. "Oh, uh...hi, Mrs. Monroe. Sorry about what I said."

Mrs. Monroe laughed and said, "Okay, Vanessa, but how about calling me 'Donna'? It makes me feel ancient when you are so formal with me."

"Okay, Donna," Vanessa said. She looked around the room. Something was bothering her. She looked at Molly. She did remember being in this room before.

Molly was looking at her oddly. "Are you okay, Ramirez? What's going on with your foot?"

Vanessa realized she was tapping her foot again. She wasn't sure what that was about. It just happened. "Something is missing," she said.

"What do you mean?" Mrs. Monroe asked her.

"Where's the picture?" Vanessa asked.

"What picture?" Donna and Molly said.

"I remember a picture!" Vanessa yelled. She hadn't meant to scream like that.

"Vanessa, relax…" Molly started.

"Oh, that picture," Mrs. Monroe said.

"What is she talking about, Ma?"

"Beth brought a picture of the four of you: Nick, Beth, John, and you."

Molly stared at her mother. "You know about John and me?"

Mrs. Monroe looked like she was about to cry.

Vanessa had the feeling she had screwed something up. Her foot wouldn't stop tapping.

Promises

Private First Class Dakota Hart

He had been awake for eighteen hours, and though the sky was peppered with stars, it was pitch-black in the edges of the valley. But Hart was too wired to feel tired.

He had been preparing for this all day. The explosions at the dining facility had created chaos on the camp and had initially hindered planning for the extraction. The plan had changed at least three times that Dakota knew. But he was ready for this. His skin tingled with anticipation for the fight.

The Special Ops team would be conducting the extraction. The Alpha-team Marines were simply there to clear the way out. The explosive-ordinance Marines had left ahead of their convoy to clear the Alpha Company route to the rally point.

They had stopped the convoy a mile out so that the Marines could enter on foot. They hadn't been given the go yet, so Hart was still in the gunner's seat of their M-ATV. Their driver had just left the vehicle to take a piss.

"You're awful quiet up there, Hart. Don't fall asleep on me," Lieutenant Michaelson said.

"Not a chance, sir. This M-240 doesn't feel much like a pillow." Hart tapped the machine gun affectionately as he spoke. He recalled the downed Osprey and the platoon of dead Marines, and he wanted to make the hajjis pay for what they'd done. He wished they could drive the M-ATVs in that town at full speed, just raining bullets down on them. He thought of Sergeant Hicks and of Corporals Carter and Murphy. He

pulled on the threads of anger and held onto them, coiling them around his heart like a ball of yarn, trying to make it as big as he could to edge out the fear that threatened to distract him.

The second explosion at the cafeteria looped in his head. He hoped Monroe and the others were all right. "Did you get any word on Corporal Monroe's condition since they medevac'd her out?"

"Not much. All I know is she was still alive when we left Leatherneck."

A heavy silence grew between them. It was bad enough to lose men on the battlefield. Something about a woman though – it was just harder to swallow. And he liked the corporal. She might be quirky, but the girl had grit.

"Hart."

"Yes, sir?"

"If I don't make it out of here, there's something I need you to do for me."

"You have my word, sir."

Corporal Molly Monroe

Molly woke up to an empty room, and she was glad. Ramirez had freaked out, and her mom had acted weird. She didn't understand why her mom hadn't mentioned John to her yet, unless maybe she was trying to avoid a fight about him while Molly was here. But that didn't ring true to her. Her mom looked upset.

The nurse had come in the room after Ramirez screamed at them and had taken her back to her own room. And she must have put something in Molly's IV as well, because she didn't remember anything after that.

She thought it was good that her mom knew about John. She was tired of the secrets.

They were sitting on towels at Clearwater beach, watching a volleyball game in the distance.

"We need to tell your mom," he said.

"I know. I'm just not ready for the fight," she told him.

"It's not right to lie to her, Molly. I'm really not okay with that. Why won't you give me a chance to win her over?"

"Don't you understand, John? It's not you. It's the uniform. She'll never be able to get past that."

He had touched her chin and compelled her to look him in the eyes. "Well, she's going to have to get past that. You know I'm going to marry you one day," he'd said.

Molly fell back to sleep wondering when she would see him again.

Grave Matters

Beth Bailey

*Nick had walked Beth home when they returned from Tiger
Stadium on the Fourth of July.*

> *"What made you go off on John like that, Nick?"*

> *"Why wouldn't I? She's my kid sister."*

> *"She's a big girl, you know. She doesn't need your
protection. Especially not from a guy like John. You know he's
a good guy."*

> *"That's obviously not the problem," Nick said.*

> *"Well, don't tell me it's his age. Please don't be a
hypocrite."*

> *"It's not his age, Beth. Can we just drop it?"*

> *"No. I think I need to understand this, Nick."*

> *He was quiet for so long, she thought he wouldn't
answer her.*

> *"You do remember that we lost our father because of
his job, right?"*

> *It dawned on her that she knew what he would say
next.*

> *"We are a country at war. If he gets deployed, and if
he is killed in action, it would be very hard for me. But Molly
gets so attached, and she was a wreck after we lost Dad. I
wouldn't want to see her suffer like that again."*

> *Beth wished she had realized his concerns sooner, but
she was glad he had confided in her now. "I never thought
about that, but it's probably not anything to worry about,
anyway. They are going in separate directions, between her*

*college goals and his Marine Corps ambitions. In the
meantime, just be glad she's with a good guy. And try not to
ruin your friendship while you're at it."*

*He had laughed, and he then kissed her good night at
her front door.*

Nick Monroe

Six Marines carried a casket covered with the
American flag. They were in their full dress uniforms,
every inch of which was impeccable, and they marched
in step at a steady pace. Nick walked with Beth, next to
John's brother, a few paces behind their parents. The
walk to the plot in Section 60 of Arlington National
Cemetery was slow and somber and excruciatingly hot
and humid.

Nick didn't want to think about why he was
there. He had been so worried about Molly since hearing
about her condition that he had not taken the time to
process his grief over losing his best friend. He didn't
want to deal with those emotions here in front of
everyone, so he focused on the ceremony, the military
courtesies, the tradition.

He watched the Marines as they approached the
gravesite and secured the casket to the structure over the
plot. They moved as one, without commands, and he
admired their precision. They held the flag in place over
the coffin as the chaplain spoke, and when his memorial
concluded, the officer-in-charge stepped in front of the
casket and saluted. Nick watched as the honor-guard
team fired three volleys with their rifles. Although there

were seven of them, each volley sounded like one shot. And then the bugler began playing taps.

Nick held Molly's hand. He told her it was going to be all right. He would always be there for her. Nick had not understood the meaning of taps then, but when the bugler began his solemn refrain, he had felt the impact of his loss. He had understood in that moment that he would never see his father again.

Those twenty-four melancholy notes had torn through his heart as a child, and now, seventeen years later, they did it again. He felt his face crumbling.

He watched with blurred vision as the Marines folded the flag and handed it to the officer-in-charge, who walked toward the family, lowered himself on one knee, and handed the flag to John's mother.

He said, "On behalf of the president of the United States, the commandant of the Marine Corps, and a grateful nation, please accept this flag as a symbol of our appreciation for your loved one's service to country and Corps."

Nick squeezed Beth's hand. "Good-bye, my friend," he whispered. He closed his burning eyes, and he let the tears spill freely.

Picture Frame

Molly Monroe

The glow of the setting sun over a blue horizon framed the happy couples.

The four of them shared a private yacht charter on a sunset dinner cruise along the Outer Banks. Nick and Beth were smiling at the camera, but John and Molly only had eyes for each other. Her alluring smile suggested a girl newly awakened by love's first touch. It was Memorial Day weekend, and Molly had given herself to John completely only hours before.

She had believed she would always be framed in this moment. She believed she would one day be his bride.

Donna Monroe

Donna sat in the hospital recliner as Molly slept, staring at the picture of Nick, Beth, John, and Molly. She had taken the picture down and placed it in her bag after John was confirmed dead. She, Nick, and Beth were at the Fisher House when they had learned that he had passed away in Germany. John had been declared brain-dead shortly after his family had arrived. They had said their last good-byes and then had taken him off life support.

She was worried about Nick. If she hadn't been so consumed with Molly's condition since this nightmare began, she could have shown him more empathy for the loss of his best friend. Despite all the new revelations about John and Molly, she had always thought he was a very nice, polite young man. And she knew how close those boys were. Her heart broke for Nick. And she felt the deepest sympathies for John's parents. If it weren't for Molly's condition, she would have wanted to attend his funeral with Nick and Beth.

Donna had no idea what to do. She felt that young man's loss more now than ever. Knowing that Molly had loved him and now remembered him, made this so much more difficult. Should she keep quiet so that Nick could be the one to tell her? Or should she let that other young Marine, Dakota Hart, be the one to do it?

She placed the picture back on the ledge by the window. There was no need to hide it anymore.

Donna dabbed her eyes with a tissue and wondered what to expect for Molly's future. She thought about the incident with Molly's friend, Vanessa. She had shown some of the symptoms Nick had read out loud to her, but it was disturbing seeing it in person. Vanessa's memory appeared mostly intact, although she had shown some minor anterograde amnesia. The nurse had explained that Vanessa was experiencing perseveration and executive-function difficulties, which made some of her strange behavior and inappropriate outbursts more understandable. Donna had been glad she had been warned, but she was still taken aback when Vanessa had obsessed over the picture.

Donna had been afraid to say anything to Molly about John. She had not known how to tell her daughter that the love of her life was gone. It brought back memories of Matthew, and it still hurt her to this day to recall his passing. So she would avoid the subject, until she couldn't any longer.

"Excuse me, ma'am?"

She was pulled from her reverie by another handsome young man in a wheelchair at the entrance of Molly's room.

"Hello," she said.

"Hi, I'm Brian," he said. "May I come in and sit with you for a while?"

"Hello, Brian. Of course. My son mentioned meeting you. I'm Donna Monroe."

Sergeant Brian Price

He had watched Mrs. Monroe staring at the picture frame. He could not see the image but had not wanted to intrude on her obvious grieving. When she placed it on the windowsill, it had taken a moment for him to realize that he recognized all four faces. It took less than that to understand the setting.

He kept his bearing as he rolled into the room. As much as he wanted to pick up the picture and study it, he tried giving all his attention to Mrs. Monroe.

"Pleased to meet you, ma'am," he said. "I've heard a lot about you."

"I hope some of it was good," she said. "The last time I saw Molly, things didn't go very well."

"Well, that's the way it sometimes is with family, ma'am. But I know she loves you a lot. She told me that you are a teacher and how good you are with children."

"She said that?"

"Yes, ma'am. She told me a lot about her pageant days too. She didn't always love being in them, but she credited you with her success."

"That was kind of her to say so, but she would have won without me, I'm sure," Mrs. Monroe said.

"Well, she is certainly beautiful, ma'am. Inside and out."

Mrs. Monroe glanced at Molly and looked like she might not agree with him. Or maybe she was uncomfortable with him saying so. He couldn't decipher her expression, so he changed the subject.

"She said you have a green thumb, too. She once described your garden in great detail to me. That was right after she killed the only living plant in our office at Camp Lejeune."

When Mrs. Monroe finally smiled, he figured it was safe to ask about the picture. He said, "May I take a closer look at the picture?"

She handed it to him without speaking.

"When was it taken?"

"A few years ago, I think," she said. "Beth brought it with her when she arrived, so I'm not certain."

Brian looked at Molly's young face and her incredible smile and felt like he was beginning to understand her so much better than he had before. Her feelings for her lover were evident. You couldn't look at the photograph without knowing they were in a serious relationship. Brian had known her for more than a year now, and she had never looked at him that way. He had been convinced they would have dated, if not for someone in her past. Seeing this picture confirmed his belief that she had loved someone and had been unable to let go.

The lieutenant—he was the one. That explained what Ramirez saw. That explained a lot of things actually.

And now he was gone. Brian's emotions clashed. The lieutenant was a fellow Marine. He was a hero. Brian had liked and respected him. He had been watching stories about him on the news and mourning his death these last few days with the rest of the country. And now his heart ached for Molly. She had known him far better than he had realized. This would bring her even more pain, and he hated that.

But it also gave him a chance. He felt hope. And he felt wrong for that.

He could feel Mrs. Monroe watching him. He handed her the picture. "Does she know yet?"

She didn't answer. Her eyes darted to Molly, in the bed behind him.

He heard the mechanics of Molly's bed, and he realized she was adjusting her position herself as he turned in his wheelchair to fully face her. She had less bandage on her face, was alert, and met him with two questioning eyes. "Know what?" Molly asked.

Brian didn't know what to say. When he looked at her, he saw everything, and he felt everything, all at once. His emotions were so out of control, he could feel physical pain in his chest. He saw the jagged welt on her cheek, her head swollen and bruised, and he still thought she was the most beautiful girl he knew. He saw the questions and the trust in her blue eyes. She looked to him for answers, but just then, he knew he didn't have any. He wouldn't look at the picture on the mantle again, but he couldn't get that expression on her face out of his head. He couldn't stop the jealousy burning in his chest or the guilt that followed it. He could feel hope on the periphery of his pain, and it made this moment more unbearable.

He looked at her and wondered: *How much of her life does she remember today? Which memories are lost to her forever? How many of them are with me? How many with him? Who will tell her that he is dead? How badly will it hurt her?*

He realized that he had never admitted the depth of his feelings to her or even to himself. He wondered if it mattered. He wondered if she would ever look at him the way she had looked at the lieutenant.

Gold Star

Nick Monroe

It was a crisp November afternoon. John's mother had prepared the traditional Thanksgiving feast, and their whole family had been in attendance. The guys had played football with some of the neighbors' kids in their large backyard until the sun went down. And then they had watched the Broncos' victory over the Giants.

John walked with Nick on his way to the car.

"You know you could crash here tonight if you wanted," John said. "I know my parents wouldn't care. They still have that pull-out sofa bed in the office."

"Nah. Ma's already mad at me for not spending Thanksgiving Day with her. I'll drive a few hours tonight, grab a room along the highway, and get there before noon tomorrow."

"Is Molly with her?"

"No. She said she had duty this weekend, so she couldn't make the trip."

"Oh."

"Have you two spoken lately?" Nick asked.

"I saw her this summer," John said. He shook his head. "I can't be around her anymore. It would ruin both of our careers."

"I don't get that," Nick said.

"It's just the way it is, bro. I'm an officer. She's enlisted. Not allowed. End of story."

"Well, that sucks. Seems like there's something you two could have done. I think she still loves you. She doesn't ever talk to me about a boyfriend. I think she would if she had one."

John's forehead creased, and he looked away. He didn't say anything.

"Well, listen. We need to plan our next road trip. We'll need to celebrate when you get back from your deployment."

"You bet," John said.

Nick sensed the conversation was over. "It was good seeing you again, John," he said. He shook John's hand with one hand, pulled him in for a one-arm embrace, and patted him hard on his back.

"Yeah, Nick. See you on the flip side, brother."

Nick got in his car to leave, and the last thing he noticed as he pulled out of the driveway was the flag with a blue star hanging from the dining-room window.

Beth Bailey

Nick had been showing her around the Michaelsons' home and introducing her to everyone he knew. Apparently, he had been there often during their college years and a few times since then.

Nick had left Beth with John's older brother, James, while he went to the bar for a drink. She and James had been sharing stories with each other, and she was glad that they had been invited to attend this reception. Although some people in the room would come to tears or dab at their eyes once in a while, most people were talking about happy times with John, as they nibbled on appetizers being offered by the waitstaff. It was not as somber an atmosphere as the burial ceremony had been.

Beth studied the lapel button she held in her hand as she listened to James explain the origins of the button. It was round with gold laurel leaves extending along its perimeter; it had a purple interior and a gold star in the center. The Marines had given it to Mrs. Michaelson, and she now understood the expression "gold-star family."

Nick arrived at the tail end of James's explanation, but Beth could tell it wasn't new information for him. "Come here; I want to show you something," he said to Beth.

Nick nodded at him as he gently took hold of her elbow, and Beth said, "Nice meeting you, James."

They weaved around the small clusters of people in conversations, until they were standing in the front yard.

"See that flag hanging in the window," he said.

It had a red border and a gold star in the center of the flag. "Yes," she said.

Nick said, "I was here last year for Thanksgiving. The last time I saw that flag hanging there, it was a blue star."

Beth looked at the lapel she still held in her hand. "Oh. It's gold now because he died?"

"Yes. The blue star is for the next of kin to display when they have family members serving in the military during war. When it gets covered with a gold star, that means the service member died in combat. The blue star is supposed to represent hope, and the gold star represents sacrifice."

"I'm starting to understand how symbolic everything is in the military," Beth said.

"Yeah. Everything means something," Nick said. "I think it gives the military community a way to make sense of the sacrifices they make...a higher calling. A sense of purpose. I think these things help some people cope."

Beth didn't respond. She understood symbolism well. It was an artistic device she and Molly had used often in their plays. She had never seen any similarities between the military and the humanities before, but she was questioning her former impressions of the lifestyle. She thought she was beginning to understand Molly's attraction to it.

Nick interrupted her thoughts. He said, "Let's return this to Mrs. Michaelson and say our good-byes. We need to get back to Molly."

Exposure

Private First Class Dakota Hart

"Hart, watch out!"

The lieutenant pushed him hard, and a blast of rocks, dirt, and debris erupted in the spot Hart had just been standing. It knocked the helmet off the lieutenant's head, and they both fell to the dirt in a tangled heap.

Hart's ears rang, and his nose burned with the smell of scorched rubber and metal, but his body and the lieutenant's appeared intact. Hart felt disoriented and dizzy. Time stretched like a rubber band as they remained crouched on the ground. Hart met the lieutenant's eyes and with a slight nod of his head, motioned for them both to crawl toward the perceived safety of the wall, instinctively seeking cover from the sustained incoming rounds that kicked the dirt into a foggy haze around them.

They remained against the wall until their balance was restored, the dizziness receded, and the small-arms fire slowed enough to determine the direction of the source.

Hart could only hear out of one ear, but when he turned to look at the lieutenant, he saw that he was laughing.

"What's so funny?" Hart said.

"The look on your face!" the lieutenant said in a fit of laughter. "I don't know…I thought we were goners, but then we weren't. And I looked up, and you looked so shocked to be in one piece, and I was thinking…we looked like we were playing Twister. We could have won some money with that video!"

Hart exhaled and could feel a grin relaxing the tension in his face. He agreed they must have looked ridiculous. He shook his head and said, "That really was a close call, sir. Thanks...you saved my ass."

The lieutenant gave him a quick pat on the back, still smiling from ear to ear, and said, "Anytime, Hart."

They both jumped when the radio squawked, "Avenging Eagle has flown the coop. Do you copy?"

The lieutenant grabbed the radio and said, "Avenging Eagle has flown the coop, copy. Birds of prey falling back, over." Then he looked at Hart and said, "Go ahead and radio the rest of the team; it's time to regroup."

"You got it, sir," Hart said. Before he even had a chance to complete the lieutenant's instructions, he watched him walk five feet from the wall to where his helmet had landed in the dirt, and as he bent down to pick it up, a bullet ripped through the side of his skull.

Corporal Molly Monroe

"Know what?" Molly said.

Brian had an odd look on his face. She wished she had been awake to hear what he and her mom were discussing. She could not guess what he was thinking, but he seemed deep in thought as he stared at her.

Neither one of them answered her question, but her ma said, "One of the Marines you worked with in Afghanistan is here, hon. And he recently asked if he could speak with you. Do you remember PFC Hart?"

Molly tried to remember. "I can't place him," she said.

Brian said, "He's an Alpha Company Marine. I think he was with you the day the Osprey went down."

He said it like he was still distracted. He was hiding something. She could feel it.

Molly said, "I don't remember that day, and I haven't run across it in my journals. Do you want to tell me about it?"

Her ma said, "I have a newspaper clipping you wrote about the Osprey crash."

Molly and Brian stared at each other, neither acknowledging her mother's statement. Molly felt like something was wrong. A tension she didn't understand was thick between them.

He finally said, "You know, I think I might have eaten something bad. I'm not feeling so great. I think I'll head back to my room now. I'm sorry I can't stay, Molly. I'll catch you later, okay?"

Molly was confused. Brian had shared several stories with her in the last few days. She watched him roll out of her room, without touching her hand or smiling at her once.

She turned to her ma to ask her what was wrong, but the words never left her mouth. She recognized the picture on the windowsill.

Her love affair with John was exposed.

Donna Monroe

Donna watched the interaction between the handsome Marine and her daughter, and she could feel the emotional pull between them. He was smitten with

Molly—that was obvious. But it had just dawned on Donna that Molly's relationship with John Michaelson was as much a surprise to him, and to her friend Vanessa, as it had been to her. She watched Molly's reaction to Brian's quick departure, and she saw her daughter's confusion turn into hurt and then understanding to guilt when she noticed the picture frame. Molly's transparency was refreshing to Donna. She felt like she could have an honest, open conversation with her, without it turning into an argument.

"It didn't really sink in until just now that your friends didn't know about your relationship with John," Donna said.

Molly startled as if she had forgotten Donna was in the room. "Oh, I couldn't tell them," Molly said. She exhaled slowly, and relaxed against her pillows.

"Why not?" Donna said.

"Because officers and enlisted aren't permitted to date. It's against the Uniform Code of Military Justice. But I didn't know that when I joined the Marine Corps. John broke up with me when I joined. And that was why he did it."

"That must have been hard for you," Donna said.

Molly shrugged. "I guess. I don't really remember how I felt then."

"You don't?" Donna said. "I thought you were getting your memory back; you've been doing so well these last couple days."

"I remember some things. But my memories are random. Disjointed. And out of order. It's like a bunch of puzzle pieces. I don't know what's missing, Ma. The only thing keeping me sane right now is them," Molly said, pointing at her journals piled up on a chair in the corner. "And Brian's pictures and stories." Molly smiled wistfully.

"It's clear that he cares deeply for you," Donna said.

Molly's smile brightened. "I know." And then she glanced at the windowsill and sighed. "I think seeing that picture hurt him though."

"I can tell you from experience, it's hard to process, hon…when you think you know someone so well and then you find out about the secrets they've been keeping from you."

"I'm sorry, Ma," Molly said.

"It's okay. I understand your reasons now. I didn't make it easy for you. He'll understand your reasons, too. But you're going to need to talk to him."

"But I don't know what to say to him," Molly said.

"Well, how do you feel about him?"

Molly said, "Whenever he is here with me, I am content. I am not afraid…I look forward to his visits."

"And you are attracted to him," Donna said.

Molly blushed. "Yes."

"So tell him that."

"I can't."

"Why not?"

"Because I think I need to sort through what is going on with me before I talk to him about feelings. I don't know how to explain it, but I feel numb in many ways. Like my emotions are locked in a box, and I can't find the key. Some random emotions pop up, like fear and anger. But love…joy…happiness…I understand them, Ma. I remember feeling them. But that feeling inside your chest. It's not there."

"I don't understand, hon. You just said you're attracted to Brian."

Molly blushed again. "I did...I am. I feel all my nerve endings when he is around. I get butterflies when he smiles. And you know those other physical responses...but that's just chemistry." Molly looked down at her sheets when she spoke. "It's different than emotion."

Donna smiled. Molly was beet red and obviously embarrassed. She didn't remember having these kinds of conversations with her daughter before. It was nice, even if it was a little embarrassing for both of them. "But it's the best when you can have both. That's what I had with your father."

"Okay. That's way too much information, Ma! The thing is, I remember dating John, and even if I can't feel it right now, I know we love each other, and he promised not to leave me again."

Donna inhaled sharply. "Oh, hon," she said. She felt like she had been kicked in the stomach. She didn't want to do this. Not after such a pleasant exchange between them. She knew she had to. She went to Molly's bed and reached for her hand. It was time for the truth. She didn't look her daughter directly in the eyes. She was afraid she might lose her nerve. "Sweetie, John didn't have a choice this time. He's gone, and he's not coming back."

Molly looked at her in confusion. "What?" she said. "He's not dead."

Donna nodded her head. "He is," she said.

Molly looked shocked. Surprised. Angry. Donna couldn't tell. But she did not cry. "Tell me what happened, Ma."

Donna opened her mouth to explain. But the words wouldn't come. She was crying. She cried for her daughter and for her son. And for the family of the polite young man she wished she had made an effort to know better.

.

Last Words

First Lieutenant John Michaelson

Dear Molly,

I'm sorry! I wish I was there to tell you this in person, but if this letter has been delivered, then unfortunately, things haven't gone according to plan.

It' only been four hours since I watched the medevac take you away. I haven't stopped thinking of you since. I've carried on conversations outwardly, while my memories of us, of you, have played like a movie clip in the corner of my mind. There have been a few times when I've stopped the reel, and thought about things I wish I had done differently. Like pushing you away after you enlisted. But there is no changing the past now, is there?

I remember thinking I should be the one to protect you. Right now though, I can't shake the thought that you are the survivor among us, and the irony isn't lost on me.

I've thought about our talk last night, and I've realized how much of yourself you have always kept hidden; how much of yourself you've protected from the world. I've always thought you were as beautiful on the inside as the outside. I believe that even more today. But I've also learned that even with me, you were holding back pieces of yourself.

If I have anything left to offer you, it's this: Quit acting, Molly. Be yourself. Take off your masks. You don't have to pretend to be someone else. You don't need Shakespeare to be witty. It's not your uniform that makes you strong. You have proven to be resilient and ambitious on your own. And you don't need anyone — not your mother, your brother, or me — dictating your life for you.

A couple of months ago, I sent Nick a different letter to deliver to you, in case I didn't return. But don't bother reading it. Although I told you that I still loved you, which will always be true, I gave you the same old excuses about why we couldn't be together. It's a lie, Molly. I didn't even try to find a way to make it work. I just gave up on us. I should have tried. And I should have supported your decision. These are my biggest regrets.

You are a great Marine, Molly. Don't let anyone tell you otherwise, to include yourself. I'm so proud of you. I'm sorry I didn't say that sooner.

You're the only girl I've ever loved, and I wish we had our whole lives to spend with each other. But, if this is my destiny, then my final wish is that you find love again. I want you to be cherished. I want you to be loved. I want you to be happy.

But please don't forget me. As long as you remember, then my life will have mattered.

Yours Always,

John

Private First Class Dakota Hart

"He saved my life," Dakota had told them.

He was in Corporal Monroe's room. Her mother, Nick, and Beth were there, too. They had asked what happened the last time Dakota saw the lieutenant, and he had told them.

"I keep thinking if he hadn't saved me, he would still be alive. His helmet wouldn't have fallen off," he said.

"It was his decision to save you, and it was a good one," Nick said. "He would have made the same decision again, given the chance."

"I should have gone for his helmet, since I was still protected. I just watched him and did nothing," Dakota said.

"Do you think this would have created a different outcome?" Mrs. Monroe asked him.

"I think if I had been as quick-acting as he was, maybe I could have saved his life," Dakota said.

"But you don't know that, dear," Mrs. Monroe said. "Nothing you did *caused* his death." She looked at her son when she spoke. "It is not healthy for you to blame yourself for other people's actions." She looked at Dakota now. "You didn't pull the trigger on the weapon that killed the lieutenant. You need to remember that."

"Yes, ma'am," Dakota said. He couldn't argue with her logic, but it didn't stop the nagging feeling in his chest. "I need to get back to my room, but I promised him that I would deliver this to Corporal Monroe." He handed the letter to the corporal. "I hope you heal quickly, Corporal."

She smiled at him, like a plastic doll, with no light behind her eyes. He studied the scar on her face and knew that it would always be with her, but that wasn't the scar that mattered most.

She nodded and whispered, "Thank you," and he supposed she knew what he meant.

Epilogue

It had been Nick's idea. "We need to do a road trip with all your friends," he had said.

"And me!" Donna had said.

So Brian and Nick had spent the last several weeks arranging it all. Nick had rented a ten-passenger van and had driven with their ma to North Carolina. All the others had met at Camp Lejeune. It had been a lively ride to Virginia.

Baptiste and Jankowski had filled them in on the remainder of the deployment. Hart had described every detail of his three surgeries since the summer. Vanessa had a notebook that she referred to frequently, and she took pictures and videos with her phone often to help keep from repeating herself. Brian and Baptiste had figured out how to distract Ramirez from her foot-tapping tic (which, they now knew, indicated her level of anxiety)—usually by making her laugh. Nick and Beth had filled everyone in on their wedding plans, while Donna would randomly interject her ideas on the subject.

Molly and Brian sat in the back of the van, watching the others in their animated conversations. Molly scribbled notes in her journal, while Brian would take random snapshots. When they weren't actively engaged in other activities, he held her hand.

Once, when she had turned to look at him, his eyes and smile had widened, and his dimples became more prominent.

"What?" she said.

When he hesitated and shook his head, she poked him in the ribs. "C'mon, Brian."

"The look," he whispered. "You gave me the look."

She felt warmth radiating inside her chest, and she recognized the feeling. "I love you," she said.

She pulled him close and kissed him.

***

Molly and Vanessa could walk but not on a trip this long. Hart could only walk with crutches. They had several stops to make though, so they had all conceded to the wheelchairs. Brian was healed, but he still walked with a slight limp.

Nick and Beth led the way, with Donna and Baptiste walking behind them. Baptiste pushed Vanessa in her wheelchair, Brian pushed Molly, and Jankowski pushed Hart behind them. They would be making three stops at Arlington to visit Lieutenant Michaelson's, Corporal Murphy's, and Corporal Carter's graves. They wouldn't be able to see Sergeant Hicks today because he had been buried in Texas. Brian and Molly would be flying there on their own the following afternoon.

When they reached the lieutenant's grave, they formed a semicircle around it.

They all became quiet. Only the chirping of the birds could be heard for several minutes.

Nick spoke first. "We needed a road trip, John. So we decided to take one with you." He looked at the Marines and said, "Tell me something I don't know about him."

Hart spoke up first. He told them about the first time in the rear that the lieutenant had PT'd with the platoon. They didn't know he was into CrossFit, and he surprised them all with a circuit course with kettlebells, tractor tires, plyo boxes, and jump ropes. "He showed the muscle heads how it's done," Hart said. "No one else in the platoon could keep up with him."

"I saw him in the Combat Operations Center once," Jankowski said. "He had been given some of those random cards from a hometown elementary school. He was writing to the kids. Not typing. They were handwritten notes. He was artistic, too. He drew cartoons of tanks and Marines in uniform. He took his time with the letters. I thought it was really sweet."

"He was on one of our missions," Baptiste said. "I saw him passing out candy to the kids. And bottles of water. I don't think he was supposed to on that trip because of the area we were in. Those kids seemed to really like him, ya know?"

"I saw him kissing Molly," Ramirez said. "I thought he was a D-bag and she was a hypocrite."

No one spoke. They were used to Vanessa's lack of filter by now. But Molly was still embarrassed. She glanced at Brian, and he looked away.

"I'm sorry, Molly," Ramirez said. "I was a jerk. I should have talked to you about it."

Molly looked at Vanessa and smiled awkwardly. She knew Vanessa would start foot-tapping again if she didn't keep their conversation light. "It's okay, Vanessa. I think I would have been mad if I had been in your shoes too. Besides, we didn't really get a chance to talk after that."

"I knew he was keeping you away from his missions," Brian said quietly. "I didn't know why. But I knew. I didn't want you out there either."

Molly stared at Brian and shook her head.

"I knew, too," Nick said. "He told me in a letter."

Molly read the headstone of John's grave. She silently told him that she forgave him. She looked at her brother and then at Brian. "I forgive you both. But this has to stop."

"You're right, Molly," Nick said. "But please tell me you understand. We are programmed to protect the women in our lives."

"It didn't do any good, anyway," Brian said. "We weren't safe on the camp either."

"Exactly!" Molly said. "We could die in a car accident today. I appreciate your concern. I really do. But life can be ugly. It's not always fair. I need you both to trust me to make my own decisions." Then Molly looked at her mom. "Whatever their consequences may be, they are my decisions to make. Not yours."

Her ma nodded her head, and Molly knew they had an understanding.

Molly cleared her throat and said, "Thank you for your letter, John. I want you to know I'm not pretending anymore. I know my path now. It's been a part of me all my life; I just never recognized it. Whether in the Corps or not, writing is my calling. And I'm going to use it to make sure you and the others are never forgotten. Your life matters. Your story will be told."

Squirrels scampered up a nearby tree. A flock of birds took flight. The friends solemnly contemplated the life of Lieutenant John Michaelson: A hero to some. A friend to others. A brother to all called Marine.

Baptiste helped Molly, Vanessa, and Hart to stand. Then they all stood at attention as she began to sing, "From the halls of Montezuma, to the shores of Tripoli…"

***

When they prepared to leave, Brian asked Donna to push Molly's wheelchair, and he lingered behind. When the others were out of earshot, he cleared his throat and whispered, "She is cherished, sir. I thought you would want to know. Semper Fi. Rest in peace."

About the Author

Sondra Sykes Meek is originally from Florida, but she has lived in several locations in the United States and abroad. She is a wife and mother of two, a retired Marine Corps Master Sergeant, and a Project Manager in the Defense Industry. She earned a Master of Fine Arts in Creative Writing, and has several stories in various stages of progress. She hopes to write full-time one day, but for now, she writes in the spare, quiet moments of her life.

Sondra wrote and published *Model Marine* to reveal the courage and sacrifices of Marines and their families. She wanted to offer readers another kind of hero: someone who is not supernatural, immortal, or from the future. Although the events of this story are fiction, the setting and characters are influenced by her experiences as a Marine. The narrative is as authentic as it can be without excluding civilian readers. The protagonist is named after a Marine Corps icon, "Molly Marine." This is especially relevant now, as 2018 marks 100 years since the first woman joined the United States Marine Corps.

Sondra hopes all readers enjoy this emotional journey of love, loss, and sacrifice. There are real heroes hidden within the pages of her debut novel. She invites you to meet them, love them, and remember them.

***

Dear Reader:

Reviews are important to authors! If you enjoyed reading Model Marine, please take a moment to place a review on Amazon and/or Goodreads.

Amazon:
https://www.amazon.com/Model-Marine-Sondra-Sykes-Meek-ebook/dp/B078ZZQWDT

Goodreads:
https://www.goodreads.com/book/show/37936605-model-marine

CPSIA information can be obtained
at www.ICGtesting.com
Printed in the USA
LVHW05s0247120918
589891LV00001B/372/P

9 781548 687274